BETWEEN TWO KINGDOMS

JOE BOYD

Standard
PUBLISHING

Cincinnati, Ohio

Published by Standard Publishing, Cincinnati, Ohio
www.standardpub.com

Copyright © 2010 by Joe Boyd

Printed in: United States of America
Project editor: Laura Derico
Cover design and interior illustration: Michael Erazo-Kase
Interior design: Dina Sorn at Ahaa! Design

ISBN 978-0-7847-2358-6

Library of Congress Cataloging-in-Publication Data

Boyd, Joe, 1973-
 Between two kingdoms / Joe Boyd.
   p. cm.
 ISBN 978-0-7847-2358-6 (perfect bound)
 I. Title.
 PS3602.O9324B47 2010
 813'.6--dc22

                                       2009054196

15 14 13 12 11 10   1 2 3 4 5 6 7 8 9

To Debbie, Eli, and Aidan
May we grow eternally seven together.

And to Mom and Dad
Thanks for a childhood worth never leaving.

Fairy tales are more than true; not because they tell us that dragons exist, but because they tell us dragons can be beaten.
—G. K. Chesterton

My dear Lucy,
I wrote this story for you, but when I began it I had not realized that girls grow quicker than books. As a result, you are already too old for fairy tales, and by the time it is printed and bound you will be older still. But some day you will be old enough to start reading fairy tales again.
—C. S. Lewis, from the dedication of
The Lion, the Witch and the Wardrobe

TWO KINGDOMS

The Upper Kingdom

M ount Basilea pierced the highest clouds in the sky, rising up sharply from the center of a large island in the middle of a vast ocean. The edge of the island was ringed all around with low, rocky hills and cliffs, which made the lower valley regions of the island impossible to see and barely approachable by any seafaring travelers, had any dared venture that way. On one side of the mountain, the thick, dense forest that began somewhere in the clouds gave way about two-thirds of the way down to barren lands and the harsh, angular shards of an obsidian landscape. But on the other side of the mountain, fertile foothills with quilted croplands hinted at civilization somewhere behind the rocky ring. And above the lush forest, glittering like a rare jewel set upon a velvet pillow, shone the crystal towers and golden walls of the Palace of the Great King.

The palace marked the heart of this mountain kingdom—the Upper Kingdom, which had no beginning, but always was. The Great King, whose name was ancient and unpronounceable, ruled the entire expanse of the Upper Kingdom—every tree and animal, every stream and pathway. His son, the Good Prince, faithfully served his father with eternal devotion. The King and Prince had justly and lovingly ruled their subjects for as long as anyone could remember.

Tommy was one of the subjects. Seven years old, with wavy blond hair, pale skin, and blue-green eyes that sparkled when he spoke, Tommy could not remember ever living anywhere but in the Upper Kingdom. And he did not know anyone, apart from the King and Prince, who was either older or younger than he was. Everyone in the Upper Kingdom, boys and girls alike, remained the same age— eternally seven.

Mary was another seven-year-old in the Upper Kingdom, but she had not lived there as long as Tommy. She wore pretty sundresses and frilly socks, and liked to keep her long, brown hair in pigtails. She also loved to explore the forest and build tree houses.

Every morning began the same way for Tommy and Mary. They awoke in their sleeping chambers within the Palace of the Great King and walked through a series of winding interior passageways leading to a huge outdoor patio. The children of the King gathered daily in the morning sunlight to eat breakfast together at tables on the patio. Tommy and Mary always met, just after sunrise, at the third table from the palace entrance. From there, they could see most of the King's grand gardens.

With the other children, they always shared the same breakfast: warm, chewy, chocolate-chip cookies and glasses of cold milk. Once breakfast was finished, everyone played hide-and-seek in the gardens of the palace and afterward took naps among the flowers and trees.

Many of the children never left the palace grounds, but Mary and Tommy always had other plans.

Most days, the two friends packed lunch in a big basket, collected their tools, and walked halfway down the mountain into the heart of the Great Forest. Tommy loved the Great Forest even more than the King's palace, because it was so big. As he and Mary walked the soft, moss-covered paths winding into the deepest parts, he dreamed of secret places in the forest he had yet to explore and listened as Mary told stories.

"So then, this traveler tried to climb the mountain, but every time he went higher and higher, he fell harder and harder, until his body was so weary he couldn't climb another step and he came back down, sad and angry all at once. And then he tried to cross the creek, but every time he waded in, the waters grew faster and faster until the current threatened to sweep him away altogether, so he turned back and fell on the bank, tired and sad and angry all at once. And then he tried to cut through the forest, but every time he stepped much past the first line of trees, the branches and brambles grew thicker and thicker until he couldn't push his way through, so he ran away from there into a field, where he laid himself down on the soft grass, defeated and tired and sad and angry all at once. And there, just like that, was where the Prince found him. And do you know what the Prince said?"

"No, what?" Tommy loved the way words fell so easily from Mary's mouth.

Mary laughed. "The Prince said, 'You've been looking so hard to find your own way, you forgot to look one place.' Then he said not a word, but his eyes drifted up. And there, perched in a tall tree not far from the place where the man had begun to climb the mountain, and to cross the creek, and to cut through the forest, was a stunningly beautiful, massive zizzelle—one of the trained breed that the ancients used to ride. The man raised his arms and in a moment— Oh! Tommy, look—we've made it here already!"

Just ahead of them, in a small clearing deep in the middle regions of the Great Forest, was the tree house they had been building for the last several weeks. Every day, Tommy gathered tree limbs and cut wood with his small axe. Then he tied his rope around the stack as best as he could and dragged the bundle back to Mary, who carefully nailed the pieces into their places in the tree house. Already they had a ladder, a floor, and three walls. They worked like this until lunch, then after fueling up, they started the building again.

One night after they had made their way back to the palace and had their dinner, Tommy and Mary took their bowls of mint chocolate-chip ice cream and sat down on the grassy hill in front of the palace. Mary, chattering as she ate, didn't notice right away that Tommy wasn't eating his dessert. ". . . I think the blue birds must eat more than the brown ones because they always have worms in their mouths and the brown ones only walk around looking for worms— Tommy? What's the matter? Your ice cream is melting."

"The matter? Nothing's the matter. It's just that, I mean, I won't be able to meet you for breakfast tomorrow."

"Why not?"

"I'm going away, Mary. We won't be able to eat together or play with each other—just for a little while—but I will be back, and then we'll walk and talk . . . and finish the tree house together."

"Why? Why are you leaving?" Mary started lining up the chips in her ice cream. "I've heard some of the others tell stories about people who went away . . . and never came back. Where will you go?"

Tommy pulled up some blades of grass. "To the Lower Kingdom, in the valley beyond the Great Forest."

"The valley? You're going there? But everyone says that we aren't ever supposed to leave the mountain." Mary's normally calm, low voice sounded tight and high. "They say that if you go to the valley beyond the Great Forest, you'll fall under the spell of the Dark Prince— you'll get old and sad and you could even . . . you could . . . *die.*"

"It's only kind of true. The Dark Prince is real, I know, though I've never seen him." Tommy shuddered a little. "And people in the valley do get older and they do get really sad sometimes. And you're right. They can die. But it's different for us kids down there. We only go down when the Prince leads us. It's weird. They can't see him the same way we do, but some of them can feel that he is there. They can see us though."

"So you've been there before?"

"Once. A long time ago."

"Did they try to hurt you? the old people?"

"No, they mostly just ignored me, but even if they did do something to hurt me, the Prince says getting hurt isn't the worst thing that can happen to a person."

"So you might die!"

"No, I'm not going to die. I'll always be seven years old, just like you." Tommy looked back at the light shining through the palace windows. "The Prince says that sometimes people get hurt so bad that they have to come back here to the palace, but they can get better—maybe even better than they were before."

"Will I ever have to go down there?"

Tommy swirled his melting ice cream around in his bowl. "Maybe you will," he said. "Maybe someday you will go down to the valley. The King himself might call you into his throne room and tell you it's your time. And you'll know he's right—even if it's scary. But once you go—once you go just once—you will want to go back again."

"You *want* to go on this trip?"

"I need to go back," said Tommy. "I have to finish something."

"What does that mean?"

"I met someone on my first trip—Bobby. The Prince says that Bobby needs me right now."

"So why can't the Prince help him?"

"I don't think it works that way." Tommy watched a fly getting stuck in his pool of ice cream. "I mean, he can help him. He is helping him . . ."

"Is Bobby very old?" asked Mary, twirling one pigtail and brushing it against her closed eyes.

"I guess you could say that. He's as old as most everyone else down there. At least he looks like he is old, but if he comes up here, maybe he will be seven again."

Mary smiled. "Then he's almost the same age as us?"

"I hope he will be." Tommy set his bowl down and looked straight at Mary. "Will you do me one favor, Mary? Will you visit the King while I'm gone?"

"Sure, but why?"

"Just talk to him. Ask him to help if we get stuck down there."

"The King can do that?"

"I think he can do anything, Mary."

"I hope that you and Bobby will hurry home so we can finish our tree house. I will miss you." Mary left the last bite of her ice cream melting in her bowl.

"I'll miss you too," Tommy said. He stood up and pulled Mary up beside him. "But we are already friends. If I don't leave you for a little while, we might never get to be friends with Bobby. Besides, I think he will want to help us finish the tree house."

Mary's eyes glittered. "I'll see you when you get back, then. Maybe you'll have a story for me, this time."

"Yeah, maybe. Whatever happens, I'll find you—as soon as I get back." Tommy gave Mary's hand a quick squeeze and walked away toward his bedroom. He had so many questions himself, more than he wanted Mary to know. But the main one that kept swirling around in his head was the one that worried him the most.

Why had the Prince chosen him?

The Journey Below

While darkness still covered the entire Upper Kingdom, Tommy woke up and packed his knapsack with a change of clothes. He looked around at the familiar furnishings of his small chamber, trying to think. How long would he be away? After packing up a couple books and some extra socks, he began his walk through the cavernous hallways of the palace. Most other children still slept—warm and comfortable in their beds.

He passed a few newly empty rooms. They must have belonged to children who had moved from the palace into their own tree houses in the Great Forest, he thought. Tommy wondered if he would one day be sleeping in his own tree house with Bobby and Mary.

He pushed the great door open slowly, trying to be quiet. At a table at the far end of the patio sat two other children, eating chocolate-chip cookies and drinking hot cocoa with the Good Prince.

"Tommy!" the Prince called, in his deep, booming voice. "Come on over and have some breakfast. I have missed you!"

Tommy dropped his knapsack and practically ran to the Prince, giggling more and more the closer he got. The Prince wrapped his arms around Tommy and swung him in three full circles before sitting him on the table in front of the other children. "Are you still working on that tree house in the Great Forest?" he asked.

"Yes, Mary and I have almost finished it." Tommy tried to catch his breath. "Would you like to come see it when we are done?"

"Absolutely," said the Prince. "I can't wait to see it."

Tommy looked around the patio. "Are we waiting on others?"

"No, just the four of us on this trip. Tommy, meet Amanda and Luke. Amanda has been on several other trips to the Lower Kingdom, but this is Luke's first."

Tommy glanced at Luke—he didn't remember seeing him before, but there were lots of children in the kingdom. The boy had stringy blond hair and wore oversized black-rimmed glasses.

Luke pushed his glasses up on his nose. "I have been preparing for this trip for many years," he said. "I have read many books about the Lower Kingdom, and I have talked to many people who have been there. I am sure that our journey will be a success."

Tommy tried to hide his surprise at Luke's confidence. He turned to the girl with curly, auburn hair, who seemed to be shivering. He had bumped into Amanda in the hallways a few times, so her face was familiar, though he had never spoken to her. "Are you ready to go too?"

"I think so. Every trip is different. You will stay right beside us like before, right?" She peered up at the Prince.

"I will be with you as long as you need me, Amanda. I'll never leave you alone." The Prince laid his hand lightly on the intricately carved hilt of his sword—the Dunamas—that was strapped in its scabbard tightly to his left side. Tommy's eyes rested there too. He had never seen the Good Prince actually use the sword. He wondered what it looked like.

The Prince's voice cut through his thoughts. "Now, Tommy, run back and get your knapsack. Let's go!"

The Prince led the children deep into the Great Forest. Luke marched ahead on his own. Amanda walked away on her own as well, stopping every now and then to pick some wildflowers. Tommy thought he could hear her talking to herself as she went. He decided to hang back with the Prince.

"Well, Tommy, how are you feeling? Are you ready for this task?" the Prince spoke seriously, but he smiled as he looked down at the rather sober-looking boy beside him.

"I think so. At least, I thought so. There's just something I don't understand," Tommy said. "I don't understand why Luke is so . . . so confident. And why Amanda still seems so afraid after being down so many times before."

"Well, what about you, Tommy? Are you confident, or afraid?"

Tommy snagged a long stick and dragged it behind him on the ground. "I guess I just haven't thought enough about it to be too confident or too afraid. I just came today because you asked me to, and because I want to help Bobby."

The Prince looked down at his young learner, now using the broken limb as a walking stick. "That's why I wanted you to come today, Tommy. You always do what I ask. That's what I look for in a leader."

"But you're the leader, not me."

"That's my point," said the Prince. "You never forget who to follow. That's part of what makes a great leader. Believe it or not, many children just can't understand that."

"But I'm not a leader," Tommy said. "I've never done anything really, except build half a tree house with Mary."

"A person can be a leader long before he has the occasion to lead, Tommy," said the Prince. "Come on, let's find Luke and Amanda before they wander off in the wrong direction."

Tommy and the Prince found their companions just as the forest gave way to a vast, grassy field filled with daisies. From the opening in the trees, they could see the Gate of Separation in the distance, the entrance to the Lower Kingdom—an iron gate covered with vines and flowers, standing alone in the middle of the field.

Luke ran ahead to the gate and waited for the others.

The Prince's expression grew more intense. "I must be the first to pass through," he said. "Remember that the people in the Lower Kingdom are just like you, except that many of them are old and sad and very confused. Talk to any of them you wish, but learn to speak in a way that they will understand. And listen to their stories. Many of them will see you as you truly are, but a few may not like you at all. You will be able to see and hear me, but they will not. I will tell you what to say, so be careful to listen to me at all times."

"Will the other prince be there again?" asked Amanda.

Tommy had never seen the Dark Prince of the Lower Kingdom, but he had heard terrible and frightening stories about him. He stared at the dark bars of the gate, waiting to hear the Prince's answer.

"No, sweetie. He is not in this part of the city today." The Prince grabbed the girl's hand. "He is in his palace . . . planning something. All the more reason for us to get down there now. So, are we ready to pass through the gate between kingdoms?"

"Yes, sir," Luke stood at attention, just behind the Good Prince. Amanda scooted closer to the Prince, holding tight to his hand.

"Tommy?"

"I'm ready."

The Prince closed his eyes and walked through the gate with Amanda. Luke went through next, then Tommy. For a moment Tommy felt dizzy and confused. He instinctively looked back—but the gate and field of daisies were gone. There was only a heavy metal door, rusty and half-covered with illegible graffiti, in the side of an abandoned brick building.

"We've crossed over," Amanda said to no one in particular.

Tommy looked around the noisy, busy street. The city seemed a little smellier and dirtier than he remembered. He saw old people trudging along from one place to another, never acknowledging one another. Some of them, in a hurry, muttered curses under their breath as they pushed through the crowds. Others leaned lazily up against buildings or slumped on well-worn benches. Not many kids lived in the Lower Kingdom, but those who did often seemed strangely on their own. Some in torn, stained clothes were playing unattended in the streets, dodging vehicles as they came along. A loud, clanging sound throbbed in Tommy's head—construction of some kind going on somewhere in the factory district. He was struck by a feeling he had had the first time he visited the Lower Kingdom. Even though everything before him appeared real, he couldn't help thinking it wasn't—this world lacked the substance, the brightness, the solidness of life up on the mountain. It was just a shadow of the Upper Kingdom.

Almost everywhere they looked, they were met by gray, stony expressions. A thick, brown haze hung over the city.

Tommy suddenly felt a sharp pain in his stomach and bent over. "I'm gonna throw up."

"Prince! Tommy's sick!" Amanda cried.

Tommy clutched at his belly and leaned against a wall, trying to remain standing. The Prince placed his hand on Tommy's back. "It will pass, Tommy. This has been happening lately. Your body is adjusting to the climate. The air here is bad, and getting worse every day. Just breathe. You have to let your lungs accept the air."

Tommy grunted. "Maybe—shouldn't be here. Go back?"

The Prince closed his eyes and put both hands on Tommy's head. "There will always be reasons to go back, Tommy. You can always go back if you want, but you can't always come in."

The pain eased. Tommy rubbed tears from his eyes and took a deep breath.

Amanda touched his shoulder and whispered, "It's OK. The same thing happened to me last time."

The Prince kissed her on the forehead and pointed toward the street. "There they are. Go ahead and ask them to play."

Amanda approached two little girls playing with rag dolls. "You wanna play with me on the sidewalk?"

The Prince looked down at Tommy. "Are you ready to look for Bobby?"

"Do you know where he is?"

"I think I do."

As Tommy followed the Prince, he realized that Luke was gone. "What about Luke?"

"He ran off," said the Prince. "He ran ahead on his own while you were sick. Luke has much to learn—he should have stayed and watched Amanda."

"Amanda? But she's so nervous and scared. What could Luke learn from her?" asked Tommy.

The Prince turned around and motioned toward the sidewalk where they had left the girls playing. "Look."

Tommy couldn't believe what he saw. Amanda was opening the rusty metal door and beckoning the two little girls to follow her.

"They have accepted her invitation," said the Prince. "Their names are Samantha and Kelly. Amanda met them on her last journey here . . . the same way you met Bobby."

"I want to see Bobby now," said Tommy.

"So do I, Tommy," said the Prince. He turned toward a diner across the street. "Follow me."

Finding Bobby

A small, battered bell on the door jingled a flat greeting as the Prince and Tommy entered the tiny diner, but neither the stoop-shouldered waitress nor the grimy cook behind the counter bothered to acknowledge them. Scowling men and women, drinking coffee and smoking, glanced up and then away as the bell sounded. A few stared at Tommy, wary of a new face.

Even those who sat together seemed alone.

"Over there." The Prince nudged Tommy with his elbow and pointed to a small square table in a corner.

Bobby! Tommy felt pangs of joy and then dismay. Bobby looked older. Thirty, maybe? His dark skin seemed more lined than Tommy remembered, and his eyes more resigned. With a long sigh, he took a swig of coffee and extinguished a cigarette in an ashtray already full of butts and ashes.

"Go up and say hello to him," said the Prince in a low voice.

"Will he remember me?"

"I'm sure he will. But you need to remember that he sees things differently from you."

Tommy turned and stared up at the Prince. "Huh?"

"I did not explain this to you much on your last journey, but sometimes down here people will see you as a grown-up, even though you are still seven," said the Prince. "And sometimes you will appear to be seven. It's nothing you can control, so just be you—be Tommy—and Bobby will see what he needs to see."

Tommy shuffled toward Bobby's booth, trying to avoid bumping into the surly waitress. "Bob? Hey, Bob!" He remembered that people in the Lower Kingdom liked to shorten their names.

"Tom? Hi! Sit down! It's been a while. Where have you been?"

Tommy sat in the chair opposite Bobby. "I, um . . . well, I've been back in my hometown. I'm just visiting here today. I . . . I sure am glad we ran into each other, though." He thought that he ought to order something and held up his hand as the waitress approached their table with a steaming pot and mugs. "Coffee, please."

"It is good to see you too, man," Bobby said.

Tommy added sugar to his coffee and then fiddled with his spoon. The Prince had taken a seat at the table. "Ask Bobby about his work," he prompted.

"How's work going, Bob?"

Bobby laughed, but Tommy thought his laugh sounded like he wanted to cry instead. "It's not really going at all, Tom. I was laid off last week . . ."

"Tell him you understand," said the Prince.

"But, I don't understand," Tommy said softly.

"Me neither, Tom—course, I don't understand much of anything right now." Bobby stared out the window.

"You do know, Tommy," said the Prince, and he covered Tommy's hand with his own.

As the warmth of the Prince's hand enveloped his own fingers, Tommy shivered. A thousand images flooded his mind. Childhood. School. Family. A wedding. Faces smiling. Then disappointment. Tears. Anger. Failure.

Tommy shook his head, trying to get rid of the ache that had started growing behind his eyes. "Is this all . . . true?" he asked.

The Prince squeezed his hand and let go.

"Is what true, Tom? Are you talking to me?"

"Sorry, Bob," Tommy said. "I just . . . well, your story brought back a lot of memories. I've lost my job before too. A few times, actually. Couldn't blame anyone but myself, though."

"What do you mean?"

Tommy rubbed the hand the Prince had held. "I was pretty selfish," he said. "I didn't have many real friends . . . you know, I was all about what I was going to do. I had all these plans. But one day everything changed."

"What happened?"

Tommy saw so much pain in Bobby's eyes. What were the right things to say? "Well, it all happened right here in town. A friend told me about . . . another place."

"You used to live here?"

"Yeah, for a long time I did."

"Got a job somewhere else? Maybe that's what I should do . . ."

"Not exactly, Bob. I left because I met someone."

"A girl?"

Tommy laughed. "No."

"What then?"

"This is where you're gonna have to trust me," Tommy said. "I met a king."

"You met a king?" Bobby chuckled. "What does that mean? A new boss?"

Tommy told his story to his friend. As he talked, he remembered more about his days in the Lower Kingdom. How he had grown up always wanting to be the best at everything, to make his parents proud. How he had done whatever he could, including stepping on anyone in his way, to be number one. How his desires had ultimately led him to lose everything—his jobs, his place in the community, his relationships, his home.

"Then one day," Tommy said, "I was just sitting alone, nothing to do, nowhere left to go. And a man came and invited me to his house for dinner. That was all. Something about him scared me to death, but there was something else about him that made me want to say yes. That was the best dinner I'd had in years . . ." Tommy continued to talk, telling how it took some time, but eventually he had gone to live on beautiful Mount Basilea, in the Upper Kingdom. "And that's home to me now. The Great King and the Good Prince love me like their own, and all I have to be is me. Not number one, just one of the family."

When he finished, Tommy piled up the little pieces of napkin that he had been tearing apart while he talked. He couldn't bring himself to look in Bobby's eyes again. What would he see there? Bobby must think he was crazy. It did sound crazy. An entire world of seven-year-olds, a door in a warehouse that transported people to another world, a powerful Prince who could do everything and yet not be seen?

The sound made him look up. It started low at first, like a wind whipping around the corners of a house in a storm. Bobby's sobs grew to loud weeping, and the Prince placed his hands on Bobby's chest, on either side of his heart. Most customers in the diner ignored what was going on. Some blew smoke as if to make the crying man disappear. Others stared at him and snickered as he cried. Bobby did not notice.

"I want to go back with you to the Upper Kingdom!" Bobby cried out between his sobs. "I want to meet your King."

Tommy reached out and touched his friend's bowed head. At the same time the Prince grabbed his other hand and suddenly the three of them were gone.

Tommy opened his eyes to a familiar sight, though not a comfortable one. He stood beside Bobby in the Palace of the Upper Kingdom, in the throne room of the Great King. The Prince had disappeared.

Normally Tommy loved being with the King—he always felt safe and strong in his presence. But this was different. He remembered now. He could feel the days of his life in the Lower Kingdom hanging on him. He felt dirty, ugly, and small.

"I don't belong here," he mumbled. "I shouldn't be here."

But the King took no notice of Tommy. The Great King stood and stared at Bobby with a powerful, piercing gaze. Bobby looked older now, much older than he had been even in the diner just seconds ago. "Who are you and why are you here?" the King asked, his voice echoing through the giant chamber.

Tommy had never seen anger in the King's eyes. He wanted to run away.

Bobby took a few steps back. "Please, sir, have mercy . . ." His shoulders slumped and his hair turned gray. His skin grew dry and fell into wrinkles around his eyes and mouth. He was growing older by the second.

Tommy looked in every direction for the Prince. Where was he?

Bobby's knees gave out. He crumpled to the floor under the King's stern gaze. From somewhere within the heap of sagging clothes, a wail of agony pierced the room. Tommy covered his ears with his hands and felt his stomach cramp up.

"Father, this is Bobby, and he is with me."

The voice was soft and calm, barely audible over the wailing from the man now lying on the floor. The Good Prince walked up behind Tommy, letting his hand rest on Tommy's back.

Tommy turned and grabbed the Prince's robes. "Where have you been? Where did you go?"

"I had to make arrangements for Bobby." The Prince sighed deeply and closed his eyes. Then he looked at the King. "Bobby has asked for you, Father."

The King smiled. "Bring him to me!" His voice, though still full of power, had changed from a voice of anger to a voice of love. He sat back on his throne, his arms spread open.

The Prince picked up Bobby, now a frail old man, and carried him up to the throne. The King took the aged man in his arms like a proud father holding a newborn baby for the first time. Slowly at first, and then all at once, Bobby became a child . . . a seven-year-old little boy, shaking and sniffling on the lap of the Great King. Soon he fell asleep in the King's arms.

The Prince touched Tommy's shoulder. "Let's get you to Mary. She's going to want to know what happened to you." Tommy, still shaken, grabbed the Prince's hand. At the entry to the throne room, he turned. He thought he heard something familiar.

Back on the throne, the King sang a lullaby that only he knew—a special song he sang to every new child of the Upper Kingdom.

One for Mary, One for Luke

"I must go now," said the Prince.

Tommy snuffled. "Why? Where are you going?"

The Prince pushed one of the heavy oak doors of the palace that led out to a courtyard and held it open for Tommy. "Our adventure is not over—one still remains."

"Luke! Where is Luke? Do you need me to go with you?" Tommy tried to sound brave.

The Prince knelt beside Tommy. "You are not yet ready to help Luke. Where he is, only I can go. I believe Luke has been captured by the Dark Prince of the Lower Kingdom."

Tommy's eyes filled with fear. "You said the Dark Prince of the Lower Kingdom wasn't anywhere around where we were!"

"And he wasn't, Tommy," the Prince replied. "Luke went to the Palace of the Dark Prince on his own. He thought he was doing something good, but he entered a world he knows nothing about. But don't worry, I will go and bring him back home."

"Is he hurt? Why doesn't he just come back?"

"He is hurting very badly," the Prince sighed. "And he has forgotten how to come back. But I can make him well again."

Tommy wiped his face. "Then I will ask the King to help you find him."

"That would be the right thing to do." The Prince stood and smiled. "I must leave now. Go to Mary. Tell her your story. Tell her about Bobby and all that my father has done for him." He started walking swiftly toward the stables.

"Prince!" Tommy called after him. "Thank you! Thank you for the day you . . ." Tommy looked back toward the palace. Then he ran and gave the Prince a quick hug.

"You're welcome, Tommy. I couldn't imagine the Upper Kingdom without you."

Tommy ran toward his tree house as fast as his seven-year-old legs would carry him. Question after question came to his mind with every step. What was the Prince going to do? What would happen to Luke? Why in the world had he gone to the Dark Prince? How could he explain all this to Mary? When would Bobby get here? What would Mary think of him? Should he tell Mary what he remembered about the Lower Kingdom? about his own life there? He didn't even know if he understood all of that—it seemed so strange, like it had happened to someone else. What if he told her, and she didn't understand? Worse yet, what if she didn't like him anymore? And what about her? It suddenly dawned on him that Mary had not actually lived in the Upper Kingdom for all that long. What had her life in the Lower Kingdom been like? Was she once old like he had been? Could she remember?

Near the tree house, he yelled, "Mary! Mary, I'm home!"

"Tommy?" A faint voice came from inside the tree house. "Tommy!" Mary nearly fell from the tree in her effort to get down. She ran straight to Tommy as he ran to her. They met in front of a huge oak tree and embraced with laughter.

"I missed you, Mary."

"I missed you, too. But I'm so glad you are back so soon! I thought you might have to be gone, well, a long time." Mary pulled away from Tommy, holding his hands. "Did you find Bobby?"

"Yes! He's in the palace with the Great King right now."

"Is he really old?" she asked, with a gulp.

"No, I mean, he was. But something amazing happened. I don't know exactly how, but the Prince brought him to the King, and the King held him and, and—he's seven now—just like us!"

"Really? I don't understand. Do you think he will be, I don't know, different? I mean, not just his body and skin and stuff. Do you think he'll be the same person you knew in the valley?"

Tommy took his hands away from Mary's and shoved them in his pockets. He looked at the tree house—he could see the improvements Mary had been working on. "You know, I don't really know. But I think so, sort of. Only better. Happier. That's how I feel anyway."

"What do you mean?" Mary asked.

Tommy took a deep breath. This was it. He'd have to tell her. He'd have to tell her how bad he used to be. "Well, I mean that's how I feel. I feel like I'm the same person I was. I like the same things I used to like in the Lower Kingdom. Like mint chocolate-chip ice cream, and being outside. I think some of the same things. My voice still feels like my voice and my brain still feels like my brain. But something inside is different. Better." He dared to meet Mary's puzzled gaze. "Is this making any sense?"

"Well, kind of. I just never really thought of you any other way than just how you are now. Are you trying to tell me that you used to be old?"

"Yeah, I used to be. I used to be a lot of things that I'm glad I'm not now. Listen Mary, I've got to tell you this. I don't want to—"

"You don't have to tell me anything you don't want to, Tommy," Mary interrupted. "I mean, I'll listen to anything you want to say. But you don't have to tell me anything more. You're my best friend. I don't need to know about any of the other stuff. All I want to really know is that you'll never leave me. Promise me you'll never leave me again?"

Tommy didn't know how to answer her. "I don't think I can promise that, Mary. I mean, I want to, but I have to do what the Prince asks me to do. That's kind of what I'm trying to say. I do things for different reasons now. Better reasons." He took her hand and squeezed it. "This mountain is my home. I will never leave this place for always. But maybe just for a little while."

"But why?" Mary pleaded. "All we need is here, especially now that your friend Bobby is here too."

What would the Prince say if he were here? "You're right. We don't need anything here. And you are here, and Bobby is here. But there are others. Lots of others. And they do need things. They need what we have. That's why we have to go there."

"We? You mean, you really want me to go too? Down there?" Mary started twisting both her pigtails at once.

"Once you go just once, then you will see why it's important that we go. If the Prince asked you to come with me to the Lower Kingdom, wouldn't you go?"

Mary stopped twisting her hair in knots. She started to walk back to the tree house, then stopped with her back turned to Tommy. Tommy's palms grew sweaty. What was she doing? What was she thinking? A strong breeze started blowing through the trees, making the branches scrape against their tree house. The scratching sound grated on Tommy's ears. Was Mary not talking to him now? Had he said too much?

Mary turned suddenly and looked straight at Tommy with her chocolate-brown eyes. "OK. I think I'm ready," she said. "Next time, we will go down . . . together."

Luke's Chains

M ounted on his fleet-footed white steed, the Prince flew through the Great Forest to the Gate of Separation. Where was Stephen? He should be here already. Had he been detained? He tied up his horse and paced in front of the gate, then stopped suddenly, as if listening to something. He opened the gate, and Stephen, in his shimmering, reflective messenger robes, gold-plated boots, and golden helmet, emerged from the other side.

A slender golden sword hung from his belt. He removed his helmet and bowed low to the ground. "You called for me, my Prince?" His voice was deep and calm. "I am here at your service. Your commands are my delight."

The Prince lifted the messenger to his feet and stared into his battle-worn eyes. "My servant Stephen, guardian of the children of my father, the King, I fear Luke has wandered deep into the quarters of the enemy. I trust you have been watching him in the time I have been away?"

"Yes, my lord. I know where he is."

On the other side of the gate, no one noticed the Prince or Stephen as they walked through the littered alleys toward the palace in the lower part of the valley.

They strode out from the shadow of a row of dilapidated factories.

The Prince sighed heavily as the tops of the enemy's towers came into view. "Quite deceptive in their assumed beauty, aren't they?" he remarked. "I can see why the people are drawn to them. From this distance the place looks as impressive as my father's palace."

"Yes, my lord," said Stephen. "If only some would risk the death sentence and touch the palace to discover what it is truly made of."

After a short time, the two approached the castle entrance, guarded by two burly men in leather armor and carrying spiked clubs. The guards did not see or hear the pair at all.

"This way, my lord," Stephen led the Prince around that entrance to a side door, the guards' entryway. He opened the door easily and wove his way through warren-like hallways that seemed to get narrower and darker at each turn. At last, the hallway opened up into an immense, vaulted room.

The sounds of rustling and clanking had reached their ears long before they entered this room. Now the Prince could see the source. Hundreds of men and women, mostly older than thirty, though there were a handful of teenagers and younger children, sat shackled on battered metal chairs. Their faces were masked by rusty helmets clamped down on their heads, with iron visors that covered their eyes. They were in neat semi-circular rows, radiating out from a small, black stage in the center of the room. Every face was turned toward this center point, where a light from somewhere high above beamed straight down on the only occupant of the stage.

He was a short, bent over old man, with a white beard and mostly bald scalp, a shock of white hair standing out on either side of his head, just above his ears. He wore a voluminous black velvet robe, which he constantly fiddled with and folded around his body, seemingly never comfortable with the arrangement of his limbs, or the covering over them. There was a low, grumbling hum coming from within those folds, like the drone of some ancient chant music. Beside the overstuffed chair on which he sat, a precarious stack of books, magazines, and newspapers threatened to topple over onto him. He was reading aloud.

Stephen and the Prince watched from the shadowy recesses near the entrance to the lobby. They saw no guards. No other people of any kind. Just the old man and the prisoners.

"From what I can tell, this project started—according to the time of the Lower Days—about three weeks ago. As long as he reads," Stephen whispered, "the people forget about their chains, and don't seem to mind their blindness—" Loud cheers went up from the crowd just then, as if they were watching their favorite sporting event. Some laughed. Some sat quietly, grinning.

Stephen continued. "However, once a story ends, they all begin to weep and moan, panic and scream until the storyteller begins again. This goes on, night and day, with no breaks that I have witnessed. If they fall asleep, they sleep sitting up. On rare occasions, and on no regular schedule that I can discern, they are brought very meager provisions. New 'listeners' are added every day."

The Prince spotted Luke sitting between two elderly women. He was the only child on that side of the room, though he now looked more like a teenager than a seven-year-old. He sniggered at the current tale being told.

"I was able to speak to him briefly before he was imprisoned. He thinks he was supposed to come here," Stephen whispered. "Something he researched, he said. He believes that he was meant to come here and save these people, though he would not tell me how. I gathered he considered himself some hero-not-yet-come. But now he is just here, addicted to the stories like the others." Stephen's mouth curled around the word *stories*, like he had bitten into a rotten orange—something meant to be good and sweet, but turned to bitter mush. "He weeps loudly between readings and I can feel how he longs for his home in the Upper Kingdom, but he can't break his chains . . . then he forgets his pain once the next story begins."

"Has he ever even tried to call for help?" The Prince turned to face the messenger.

"No, he is too ashamed. Too afraid to say your name here. And most of the time, he doesn't even remember your name. The storyteller's voice strangles his thoughts and clouds his mind. I've tried to speak to him, but he doesn't hear me during the stories. And between readings, it's almost impossible to get his attention, no matter how loudly I speak." The messenger's gaze settled on Luke's visored eyes.

"The more he ages, the more he will forget about me and the Upper Kingdom. Now is the time to rescue him, before it's too late." The Prince watched the storyteller turning one of the last few pages of the book that was in his hand. "When this story ends, do all that you can to delay the storyteller from beginning the next book."

"Your commands are my delight!" Stephen dashed toward the storyteller, shouting the battle cry of the messengers: "For the King and his Prince!" The storyteller had just opened his mouth to say "The End" when Stephen reached the stage. Unseen, the messenger thrust his golden sword entirely through the giant pile of books and papers waiting to be read.

A terrible chaos filled the giant chamber. The prisoners wept and yelled in agony, without the distraction of a story. The Prince rushed toward Luke, unlatched the heavy helmet, and dropped it to the ground with a clank. Luke blinked his eyes, squinting at the brightness of the light. As his eyes adjusted, he burst into tears before the face of the Prince.

"Say the word, Luke! Say the word!" pleaded the Prince, turning Luke's head toward him.

Luke wept uncontrollably, unable to speak through his tears.

Puzzled and increasingly frustrated, the old storyteller clawed at the stack of books, trying to retrieve just one.

"Luke!" The Prince's tone grew more urgent.

"I . . . I . . . I'm sorry! . . . I'm sorry," Luke spluttered, shutting his eyes tight.

The Prince leaned close to the boy, his mouth just by his ear. "Say the word," he said, in a voice only Luke could hear.

Luke's sobs slowed. He mustered a deep breath. "Help me, my . . . Prince!"

His shackles broke loose.

Stephen met the Prince's eyes as he heaved Luke over his shoulder. "Now is not the time," the Prince declared, and the messenger nodded in agreement. He removed his sword from the stack of books and kept it drawn as he led the way through the rows of moaning prisoners. By the time they reached the door, the storyteller, having recovered from his confusion, began reading again and the crowd immediately quieted.

Together the Prince and the messenger retraced their steps through the black hallways, out of the palace, and back into the city, while Luke slumped in exhaustion over the Prince's shoulder. Finally the three approached the Gate of Separation. Stephen threw the iron door wide open, and the Prince crossed into the Upper Kingdom without missing a stride.

Once in the Upper Kingdom, Luke's face softened, and his body relaxed into a deep sleep. His skin grew younger, and his lanky limbs morphed back into those of a seven-year-old child of the King. The Good Prince easily mounted his patient steed, who had been waiting by the gate. Then he repositioned Luke in his arms and gave his horse the signal to move. Stephen followed behind them as they traveled through the Great Forest toward the Palace of the Great King.

From the edge of the forest, the Prince could make out a figure on the front terrace of the palace. The Great King sat quietly, watching the path leading from the Great Forest. He clapped his hands when he spotted the rescue party and hurried out to meet them, his royal robes flying behind him.

"Was it hard to find him, my son?"

"No, your messenger led me right to him."

Stephen had fallen to the ground and removed his golden helmet at the feet of the Great King.

"Thank you, Stephen." The King lifted Stephen to his feet. "Good work, Messenger. But there are more pressing matters at this time. I need you to quickly find the old builder in the village and bring him back here to discuss our next move."

"Your commands are my delight, my king." Stephen bowed his head and raced away in a golden streak.

The King turned his full attention to Luke. "Is he well, my son?"

"He is tired but in good condition."

"May I have him now?"

The King carried the sleeping boy toward the palace, with the Prince following just behind.

A Party and a Proposal

The teeth of his battered handsaw bit into a branch of the fallen tree in a familiar rhythm. Sweat dropped from his forehead onto his left boot, planted firmly on the log. With a *crack*! the branch gave way under his weight and the blade of the saw.

Pops stepped back and wiped his brow with the sleeve of his coat. He tossed the branch onto his cart. That was a load, if he'd ever seen one.

A stern breeze rustled the forest's canopy. What sky the old man could see grew dark. He stepped over the half-salvaged fallen tree and arranged the stack of wood he had gathered. Thunder boomed. Pops startled and jumped, tipping the cart, and all the wood tumbled out. He instinctively closed his eyes and took a deep breath. Then the sky opened up and sheets of cold rain covered him.

With his eyes still closed, Pops methodically recovered every piece of wood and returned it to his cart. Knowing he had every piece, he lifted the handles and pushed the cart through the forest.

Even through the pounding rain, he could hear them. Whispers.

"Freddie?" the voice came to him.

Pops stopped and opened his eyes. "Who's there?"

"Over here," the voice whispered from within the trees to his right. Water dripped into his eyes as Pops peered in that direction.

Then he saw him. Tall and shimmering, yet half-hidden by the waving boughs of the weeping willow under which he stood.

Pops left his cart and cautiously stepped closer. "You are a—"

"A messenger of the Great King and his Prince," replied the figure. "My name is Stephen. You are being summoned to the Upper Kingdom. Your King needs you. You must go now."

Pops tried to speak, but the messenger vanished in a bolt. He stood motionless in the pouring rain long enough to replay the scene in his head; then he buttoned up his leather jacket and took off through the mud toward the Gate of Separation.

Mary arrived at the newly completed tree house first, just as the sun rose over the mountain, and began to clean. Bobby came next, arms full of a large platter of chocolate-chip cookies, which Mary placed on small plates inside the tree house. Tommy arrived last, carrying a homemade banner: Welcome to Our Tree House. He tied it between two neighboring trees along the path so that all of the children would pass under it as they came to visit.

This normally quiet part of the forest soon stirred with dozens of seven-year-old boys and girls running in and out and around the new tree house. Tommy and Bobby stood outside and told stories about how difficult it was to find everything needed to complete the tree house. Mary mostly stayed inside, offering cookies and giving what she called grand tours to small groups of boys and girls.

"Tommy?"

That call was unmistakable. "Prince? Is that you?" Tommy looked in every direction.

"Tommy, where are you?" The Prince laughed as he looked for Tommy in the sea of children.

"Over here! I'm over here!" Tommy jumped up and waved his arms over his head, though he still hadn't caught sight of the Prince. Suddenly he was grabbed from behind and thrown up in the air as the Prince placed him lightly on his shoulders. From way up there, Tommy could see all the friends who had come to his party, but he was most excited to see the Prince.

"Come and see my house." Tommy patted the Prince's head and pointed to the tree house.

The Prince whistled. "Well, look at that! Tommy, it is incredible. I have not seen such a fine house in many years in the Great Forest. Where is Mary?"

"She's inside giving tours." As they approached the front of the house, Tommy shouted up, "Hey, Mary! Come and see the Prince!"

Mary hurried down the ladder and gave the Prince a cookie.

"Thank you, Mary," the Prince said. "Your tree house is beautiful."

"Oh, thank you, Prince. We worked very hard on it."

"I helped some too, Prince," Bobby grinned, joining the group.

"I was just going to look for you, Bobby. You have all done a great job." Bobby's smile grew even wider.

The Prince leaned his head back and whispered, "Tommy, I'd like to introduce you to a friend of mine."

"Sure," said Tommy. He would go wherever the Prince wanted to take him.

The Prince lifted Tommy off his shoulders and the two walked a few hundred yards into the forest. They could still hear faint sounds of the tree house celebration as they rounded a bend in the path and came up next to a large boulder.

Tommy sucked in his breath. There on the rock sat an old man— an unheard-of sight in the Upper Kingdom. He had a gray beard and long, gray hair and wore a dirty, worn, leather jacket. Despite his appearance, he did not seem sad or scary like the old people in the Lower Kingdom. As Tommy stared, the stranger smiled, and his smile seemed to glow from within the cloud of his beard.

"Name's Freddie, but most people call me Pops." The old man reached out to shake hands with Tommy.

"Pops is a long-time friend of mine, Tommy." The Prince gave Tommy a little nudge.

"Hello, Mr. Pops, sir. It's nice to meet you."

Pops laughed so loud that anyone around would have assumed Tommy had just told the funniest joke ever heard in the Upper Kingdom. "It's just Pops, Tommy. No mister or sir."

"Pops lives in the Lower Kingdom, Tommy," said the Prince.

Tommy squinted toward the Prince. An old person in the Upper Kingdom? "But . . . I thought . . ."

"He is seven years old, just like you," said the Prince.

"No way!" said Tommy, without thinking. Pops looked more like seventy than seven. But then, the Prince wouldn't lie.

"Look again."

A seven-year-old boy with fuzzy black hair and freckles sat exactly where Pops had been just seconds earlier.

"Pops? Is that you?"

"It's still me, Tommy. I have lived a long time in the Lower Kingdom and have grown used to the old body I wear. But I'm still seven, just like the Prince said. And right now, I'm awfully glad of that." Freddie rose from his seat and stood eye-to-eye with Tommy. "I'm here because I need your help."

"What do you need?"

"I need a tree house."

"Well, you may use ours anytime you need one. I'm sure Mary and Bobby won't mind."

"Thank you, but I need a new tree house. And the Prince told me you are the person to build it."

Tommy shrugged. "Well, I'll talk with Mary and Bobby. I'm sure that we could help you—"

The Prince stopped him. "Tommy, Freddie needs you to build a tree house in the *Lower* Kingdom."

"Huh?"

"Your tree house is great here," said the Prince. "But it would be so much better there. Think of all of the people like Bobby who could hear your story if you could invite them to your house down there. Think of all of the sad and lonely people who could hear about the Great King and the Upper Kingdom while you were with them during the construction. And not just of one house, but many like it."

Tommy ran his hand through his hair as he talked, making it stand on end. "Why me? I mean, I didn't even do all the work on this one. Mary and Bobby helped so much. Why can't Freddie build a tree house with someone else?"

"I have spent all of my days building tree houses, Tommy," Freddie said. "It's time to move on. This will be my last one, and I could sure use your help."

"Tommy, it's not just the tree house. The Dark Prince of the Lower Kingdom is plotting against my father and me. Freddie— Pops—is one of my best leaders, but I need more. I need you in the Lower Kingdom right now."

Tommy tugged at his lower lip. "This is really what you want me to do, Prince?"

"Tommy, this is what you were born to do."

"Then I will do it. Pops, I will help you build a tree house in the Lower Kingdom." Tommy glanced back at the Prince. "What about Mary and Bobby? Mary hated it when I left last time."

Pops answered for the Prince. "Every good tree house starts and ends with a good team. Your first task will be to select two children of the King to accompany you on this journey. We haven't much time to delay. It sounds to me like Mary and Bobby are your choices. If they are willing, they should get ready right away. Let them know that this adventure will be exciting, but not easy. But then, most things that are truly exciting are not easy at all."

Tommy looked to the Prince with a smile. The Prince winked.

"Tommy, shall I meet you and your team tomorrow morning at the Gate of Separation?" asked Pops.

"Yes, Pops. Thank you for asking me to help you." He turned to the Prince. "Will you be there too?"

"Of course. I'll meet you and Freddie at the gate tomorrow morning."

"OK. Well, I suppose I should go talk with my team."

"That you should, Tommy. I'll see you tomorrow. I'm going to take Freddie to see my father now." The Prince hugged Tommy and then started up the path toward the palace with Pops. As they walked, the Prince placed his hand on the boy's shoulder.

Tommy watched until they disappeared into the forest before he started back. He was glad to have a few minutes to himself to think. What would he say to Bobby and Mary? What would they say? Tommy sighed. Maybe he should walk a little slower.

Tommy's Team

When the last party guest waved good-bye, Tommy said, "Let's go up to the roof and look at the stars. We can finish cleaning up later." He led the way up the ladder, and Mary and Bobby followed.

They lay on their backs with their heads touching. "What did the Prince want to talk with you about, Tommy?" It seemed Mary couldn't wait to ask that question.

"He has a friend who needs our help."

"Then we should help him," said Bobby confidently. "Any friend of the Prince must be trustworthy and good."

Mary sat up and grabbed her knees with her hands. "Who is it, Tommy? Who needs our help?"

Tommy sat up to face her. "His name is Pops. He is a tree-house builder from the Lower Kingdom. You will like him."

Mary looked like a deflating balloon. "What do you mean, he is from the Lower Kingdom? You mean he *lives* there? So he's old? Is that what you mean?"

"He looks old sometimes," Tommy admitted. "It confused me too at first. I suppose he looks old because he's been down there so long, but he is really just seven years old like the rest of us."

"Does he want you to go back down there?"

Tommy hoped Mary wouldn't get too upset. "Yes, he does. But not just me. He needs us to help him build a tree house there."

"Are we allowed to go down there?" asked Bobby. "I didn't think I would ever have to leave the Upper Kingdom. And why would anyone want to leave after spending even one day on the mountain?"

"We can go—when the Prince leads us."

Tommy rose to his feet and faced them both. He wasn't sure what to say, but he opened his mouth, and his heart spoke.

"Mary? Bobby? Do you trust me?" Tommy said.

"Of course. You are my best friend," Mary answered. Bobby nodded in agreement.

"If you really trust me, then you have to believe what I am about to tell you. OK?"

Mary started twirling her hair. Bobby was trying hard to sit still.

Tommy cleared his throat. "I must go to the Lower Kingdom with Pops tomorrow. The Prince says that this is what I was born to do. I would make the Prince sad if I didn't go, but . . . I need you—both of you." He walked around the roof as he talked. "Mary, I can't build a tree house like this one without your help. Look at how fast the three of us finished this project since Bobby joined us. I can't do this alone. I guess that I could go up to the palace and look for others who are good tree-house builders, and I might find some, but I don't want them. I want you. I want us to be a team. I want to share every minute of this adventure with you so that I don't have to spend days telling you the stories when I get back. I want us to be able to tell other people the stories of our adventure. I want to be scared with the people I trust the most and I want to celebrate with the people I love the most. So . . . will you? Will you just come with me? Pops said I need a team. He said what we're going to do will be exciting, but not easy. He said the success of the whole project starts and ends with a good team. And that's what we are—a good team. So . . . will you do this? Will you go with me to the Lower Kingdom tomorrow?"

Neither Mary nor Bobby said anything. Then Bobby got up and started climbing down the ladder.

"Where are you going?" Tommy could see only the top of Bobby's head.

"I'm going to pack. I've got a lot to do. I'll meet you back here at sunrise." Tommy thought he heard sniffling and then the soft sound of Bobby's feet landing on the ground below.

"Mary? What about you?"

"I guess I should start packing too."

"You'll go? I thought that you would say—I mean—"

"Tommy, if you were born to build tree houses, then I was born to help you." Mary wiped her eyes, smiled, and started down the ladder.

Tommy stood, alone with the stars, on the roof of his first tree house. His legs shook and his heart pounded. But still, he couldn't wait for tomorrow.

Tommy found Mary and Bobby waiting impatiently for him when he arrived at the tree house the next morning.

"I couldn't sleep anymore," Mary admitted. Tommy noticed both of her pigtails were twisted up at the ends.

"I don't think I slept at all!" Bobby said.

"Me neither," said Tommy. "Let's go on and meet Pops and the Prince."

He led his friends through the Great Forest toward the Gate of Separation, down the narrow path that stretched out of the Great

Forest into the large grassy field. At the gate, talking in the light of the sunrise, the Prince stood with Pops, who was old once again.

"Good morning!" called the Prince, waving. As if drawn by his voice, Tommy began to run and the others followed. Mary jumped straight into the arms of the Prince.

"Are you ready for your trip?" The Prince looked down at Tommy.

"We are, Prince."

"Great, Tommy. How about you, old-timer?" The Prince put Mary on the ground and turned to Pops. "Are you ready to take on these young pups?"

"I am ready, my Prince." Pops bowed low to acknowledge the Prince's royalty.

Tommy noticed the great respect Pops showed the Prince, even though they were such good friends. A new thought occurred to him—maybe it was *because* they were such good friends? But he didn't have time to think about this now.

"Shall we cross through the gate?" he asked, hating that his voice came out in a squeak.

"Not just yet, Tommy," the Prince replied, "I have something to give each of you first."

"A gift?" said Mary. "But we have all we need . . ."

"You have all you need for life in the Upper Kingdom, Mary. These gifts will help you in your work in the Lower Kingdom. Without them, well, without them you would find many things to be quite difficult. On each gift you will see a name that I have personally written. These will be your second names. Many in the Lower Kingdom go by more than one name . . . a name they are given by their parents and a second, often unspoken name that reflects their true identity." The Prince knelt down to be on eye level with the children. "Remember that only the Great King has the power to change a person's true name. Always lead the people you meet to the King."

"But how?" asked Bobby. "How do we lead them to the King who lives way up on the top of this mountain? And how do we convince them to even believe the Upper Kingdom is here if they have never seen it?"

"These are very good questions, Bobby, but you will not need to convince anyone of anything. Show them my father's kingdom; don't just tell them about it. Listen to Pops and trust your friends . . . they will help you learn how to do this. Your gifts and your new names will also help you on your journey."

The rising sun glinted on three boxes sitting next to the gate, each wrapped in golden paper and tied with silver ribbons. The Prince handed a small box to Bobby, who tore off the wrapping and found inside a beautiful golden ring with a sparkling green jewel that seemed to glow and change form in the light of the sun. Inscribed on the inside of the band was Bobby's new name: *Vision*.

Mary also received a small box. She opened it carefully, not wanting to tear the pretty golden paper. Inside she found a silver necklace with a simple, circular locket. Mary's eyes gleamed as she ran her fingers over the etched lines on the top of it. It was a drawing of some sort, beautiful curves, like waves—like flowing water.

"Open it," said the Prince.

One side of the locket held a small mirror. On the other side in golden letters was the word *Hope*.

"Oh! Thank you, Prince. It is such a pretty locket . . . and a pretty name." Mary held the chain around her neck so the Prince could fasten the latch in the back.

"You are very welcome," he said.

Tommy's box was larger. He tore the wrapping and opened the

box to find only an old brown jacket. Inside of the jacket *Humility* was written with black ink.

"Just like mine, Tommy." Pops pulled on the lapels of his jacket.

Tommy forced himself to smile. "Thank you, Prince."

"I know that it's not as fancy as Mary's and Bobby's gifts, but it is a very important one." The Prince helped Tommy put it on, as best as he could. It was clearly made for a much larger person. Why would the Prince give him a gift that didn't fit?

"You must promise me that no matter what happens, you will never take off your coat until you return to the Upper Kingdom." The Prince continued to button every button.

Mary giggled. "Your arms look very long, Tommy."

The Prince smiled too. "It will fit you better when you cross over. Just promise me that you will always wear it."

"I promise, Prince." He rolled up the big sleeves. "Even on the hottest day, I will wear my coat."

"Be careful with these three," the Prince said to Pops. "My father is incredibly fond of them."

"I will be . . . and I know. I haven't lost one yet!" Pops chuckled.

"You aren't coming with us?" Tommy had never crossed over without the Prince. How could it even be possible?

"Not this time, Tommy. I live here. I can visit the Lower Kingdom, but I was never meant to live there. But I will visit you, and my father is always watching you from his palace. Pops will teach you how to contact me. Trust him like you trust me. He has a lot to teach you."

"OK. I'll trust Pops. I'm sure we will become very good friends."

"I love you all. Be careful, but be brave. I'll see you all as soon as is possible." He hugged the children and walked back up the path and into the Great Forest.

"Let's go, Pops!" said Tommy. "I want Mary and Bobby to see the city beyond the gate."

"We're going in a different way." Pops threw his knapsack over his shoulder.

"There's another way in?" asked Mary.

"Just one other way that I know of. Follow me to the River."

The three friends looked at one another. The River?

The River

Tommy, with Mary and Bobby, trailed Pops through the big grassy field and back into the mysterious shadows of the Great Forest. Pops led the way without the help of a path or a map, clearing the brush and branches with his long walking stick.

"What do people eat down there?" Mary asked him.

"Food," he replied, with a wink and a smile.

"How big is your tree house, Pops?" Bobby asked.

"Hmm. Matters which one you're talking about. The last one I built was about the same size as yours, maybe a little bigger."

"What about the other prince?" asked Tommy.

Pops cleared his throat. "What about him?"

"Have you seen him? What does he look like? Where is his palace?" Tommy had a hundred more questions, but stopped himself.

Pops lowered his voice, and though he was safe in the Upper Kingdom, he looked in both directions before he spoke. "Well, Senkrad is remarkably . . . normal."

"Who is Senkrad?"

"That's his name," Pops replied. "At least that is one of his names." He bent back some low branches so Mary could get through easily. "Your questions are good . . . all of them. We will have time to answer every question—I hope we will have a long time. But for now, let's enjoy this walk! This is my favorite part of the Upper Kingdom coming up. A morning like this reminds me of the story of the day that the Messenger Philip battled an army of mercenary soldiers from the Lower Kingdom . . ."

Tommy walked on, listening to Pops. After a while, the trees and shrubs seemed bigger and greener and giant flowers lined the path. All the forest seemed to sway in unison as if dancing with the wind.

"Pops?" Tommy interrupted the old man's story. "Where are we? I've never been so deep into the Great Forest."

"We're nearly to the River. You should be able to hear her waters anytime now."

"Is the River scary?" asked Mary.

"Scary? Maybe at first. But once you get in, there is nothing better."

"This will be my first boat ride," said Bobby.

"Boat? There is no boat, my boy." Pops laughed. "The River is for swimmers only."

Mary gasped. "But Pops, sir . . . I can't swim. I've never even tried. We must turn around and go through the gate!"

"I agree," said Tommy. The sound of rushing water grew louder. Pops led the children around a large rock formation and past a huge evergreen tree. "We should turn around. For . . . uh . . . for Mary's sake—"

"Look, children!" Pops exclaimed. Tommy saw the River—wide, clear, and perfect. The rushing water sounded like a thousand voices, all whispering at once. Mist gently showered their faces.

Pops took a long, deep breath of the crisp, clean air. "There is nothing like it . . . there is absolutely nothing at all like this place."

Tommy looked upstream and could just barely see the glimmer of a golden roof—he realized it must be the Palace of the Great King. The River seemed to disappear somewhere beyond the gardens of the King. They were on the other side of the mountain! No one ever went here—mostly out of respect for the King. The children ran freely in the garden of the palace, but no one ever walked the paths of the King's private gardens, the gardens that wound around the mountain and up into the clouds. But the other reason no one traveled on this side of the mountain was that, just below the edge of the Great Forest, the land grew treacherous, eventually dropping off into, well, what? No child of the King knew for certain. They just knew it was a dangerous place, a place where you could fall off the mountain, out of the Upper Kingdom, away from the safety of the King.

Tommy looked downstream as far as he could see to a sharp bend in the River's path. Surely the River did not go through that treacherous country? "Does the River flow into the Lower Kingdom?" he asked.

"She starts as a small trickle, way up above the garden of the Palace of the Great King, and flows all the way down, winding down the backside of the mountain and along the edge of the Forest into the Lower Kingdom. She waters everything in her path, in both the Upper and Lower Kingdoms."

Mary knelt to stroke the petals of a purple blossom.

"I have been everywhere one would and would not want to go in these two kingdoms," said Pops, "and there is nothing more beautiful than just one flower watered by the River."

"Listen!" said Tommy. He thought he heard something strange—someone singing?

"Noise?" Pops turned.

"Like music, but more magical and beautiful. I can barely hear it."

"I don't hear anything but the water rushing," said Bobby.

"Me neither," said Mary, tying flowers from the riverbank into her hair.

Pops stood up straight, his head tilted slightly to one side. "It's her voice, Tommy. The River's voice. Yes . . . yes. She is happy to meet you."

Tommy nodded, but he didn't understand.

Pops took a few steps to stand close to Tommy. He spoke softly to him, "She's singing for you. I've never met anyone who was able to hear her voice on their first meeting. She is loud for you. You are special, Tommy. Special, indeed. The more you are with her, the clearer her voice will become."

"Pops. The River, is it . . . dangerous?" asked Bobby. His voice had more excitement in it than fear.

"Is *she* dangerous, you mean," said Pops. "I don't know everything about her, but I have learned this: she's more like a person than a thing. She can hold you, throw you, and protect you. She knows when to take you fast and when to take you slow . . . and she definitely knows if she likes you or not."

"I hope she likes me," said Mary, with a fearful look on her face.

"She will. If the Prince likes you, the River likes you. I know that for sure."

"So we just jump right in, Pops?" asked Bobby.

"Pretty much. We just jump in and away we go! Come over here by me and hold hands. Mary, you stand in the middle. It's easier if you all go in together."

"But what about our clothes?" asked Tommy.

"You go in just like you are," Pops said. "That's the only way to do it." He stepped behind them and Tommy felt a strong hand on his back. "Ready to jump?"

"Not quite yet," said Mary.

"Sure you are!"

One forceful jolt from Pops and Tommy flew into the River,

pulling Mary and Bobby along with him. Pops jumped in like a cannonball right behind them.

Cool water rushed all over Tommy's face and pulled him downstream. In a minute, he understood what Pops had meant about the River being a person with a mind of her own. She pulled him under her waters, then threw him up high into the air when he needed a breath. If he grew scared, the River calmed him down and let him float. Whenever he grew bored, the River sped up and dropped him with a force that made his stomach jump into his throat. At one point, the River pushed Tommy into Mary and the two of them, arms linked, shot way up in the air. They hit her waters again, giggling all the way. Tommy yelled, "Do that again!" and it happened! Every time Tommy asked, the River shot them skyward and caught them when they came back down.

After several hours the River slowed to a gentle flow and floated Tommy and his companions on their backs through the valley and into the Lower Kingdom. Near sunset the four voyagers were funneled into a kind of lake surrounded by huge trees. The River seemed to swirl, circling in the lake.

"Here we are," said Pops. "The Tree House Village."

The trees around the lake contained beautiful, elaborate tree houses, with doorways and chimneys and little gardens. In the middle of the village, a long wooden pier jutted into the lake from the bank. Tommy and Bobby marveled at the sight without saying a word. Mary clapped and giggled.

"This is where I have been building tree houses most of my life," said Pops.

The people milling about in the village chatted and laughed with one another. A few of the men greeted Pops from the shore as the travelers floated by.

"This doesn't feel like the Lower Kingdom at all," Tommy said. "Are you sure we are there already?"

"Don't be deceived, Tommy. This very much is the Lower Kingdom. The farther away from the River you get, the dirtier and more dangerous it becomes. Even the people who live here in these tree houses are not necessarily followers of the King. Many spend their time here fighting about the shape of their tree houses or the true identity of the King or the purpose of the River. Don't waste your time in these discussions, even if you are sure you are right. We haven't time for pointless debates."

"We'll be careful, Pops," said Tommy. "Should we get out of the River now?"

"You may get out of the River, Tommy. But the River will never leave you. Once you've been in the River, she starts to live within you. Pay close attention to how the River moves and feels now so that when you get out of her waters you will know when she wishes you to move to the left or right, up or down. The more time you spend in the River now, the more real she will be to you when you are away from her. And I fear we will be away from her for a long time on this adventure . . . longer than anyone might imagine. The more you hear her song now, the clearer you will hear it later."

"Then maybe we should just stay in for a while," said Bobby. "Besides, I love it here!" He held his nose and submerged himself.

"Perhaps we should!" Pops laughed and pushed Tommy under the water. Mary giggled and splashed water in Pops's face. And so the four children played in the circling waters of the River that flows from the Palace of the Great King.

The Long Night

Middleland

With a cool northern breeze tickling his beard, Pops slowly pushed a cart full of lumber down a mountain trail and up a slight embankment near the River. He thought about the task that lay before him. A little less than two months had passed since he led the children to submit to the power of the River. How much longer did he have to get them fully ready?

He did not know exactly what the Dark Prince was planning, but he had never seen the Good Prince as intense as during their last visit in the Upper Kingdom. In his decades of service in the Lower Kingdom, Pops had not once actually seen a messenger of the King, so to be summoned by one at the King's own command—unthinkable. But it had happened. These were not normal days.

Pops pushed his cart along the River's bank and onto the cobblestone path leading into the Tree House Village, toward the house of his old friend Roger. Roger's humble estate had served as a training center for Tommy, Mary, and Bobby, with Pops as their teacher. Pops smiled as he thought about his students. Such interesting children!—Bobby with natural bravery and courage; Mary so bright and quick to learn. And Tommy . . . Pops saw so much in Tommy—so much of himself. They had all taken in a great deal of information about the history and ways of the Lower Kingdom.

But the children had not aged at all. Funny thing, that. Most recruits began to appear as adults within a few hours or days.

Pops patted the front of Roger's tree house before he stepped inside. He and Roger had built this place long ago in the wide, old oak tree, with its massive trunk forming one wall. It was one of the first tree houses in the village.

Roger, tending the fire, nodded as Pops came in. His round, silver-rimmed spectacles set off the streaks of gray in his auburn hair. Except for the crackling of the burning wood, the room was quiet. The three children studied in wooden chairs around the fireplace.

"Pop quiz!" Pops barked. "Does anyone remember who won the Battle of Senkrad's Hill from last night's history lecture? Tommy?"

Tommy fingered the corner of his page, trying to will the answer out of his book. Mary fidgeted in her seat when she saw that Tommy did not know the answer.

"Don't remember, Tommy?" Pops asked. "How about you, Bobby? Any guesses?"

Bobby shrugged his shoulders, smiling. Memorizing names and dates was definitely not his strong suit, and he knew it.

Mary sat up straight on the edge of her chair, dying to answer. "I think I know the answer, Pops. I know!"

Pops and Roger laughed. Mary almost always knew the answers, yet always gave the others a chance to speak. "Oh? Do you have an answer, Mary?" asked Pops, with a wink. "I didn't see you there. Well, what is the answer?"

Mary spoke as if she were telling a story. "The Battle of Senkrad's Hill was won by the thirty-first legion of messengers from the Upper Kingdom under the generalship of Messenger Salma. Though many were lost on both sides, the hill was taken by Salma after Senkrad's general, the evil Etah, was destroyed by the forces of good in the summer of the twenty-second year of Senkrad's reign."

"Very good!" said Pops.

From deep within his big jacket, Tommy beamed at Mary with pride.

"Of course, as I've said before, it's not the names and dates that are so important to remember. But each of you must learn the truth of these events—you must know what was done and how and why. You never know when you might need to rely on answers of old to solve the problems of today." Pops looked around at their eager faces. "But now, put away your books. Pack up your outdoor clothes and sleeping gear, personal items. We leave in fifteen minutes."

Pops dropped his massive pack from his shoulder. "This will do just fine."

"Just fine for what?" Not once during their long trek had Tommy or any of the others asked Pops where they were going or what they would be doing when they got there. He just followed the old man, trusting his direction. But now that they were stopping, he had time to indulge his curiosity.

"Why, for camping, of course," said Pops. He raised both arms in the cool evening air, gesturing to the cleared area around them. A line of evergreens protected them from the wind on one side. On the other side a huge boulder and smaller rocks formed a kind of wall. It looked almost as if the place had been built for such a purpose. "This will be our home for the next two weeks."

"But where will we sleep?" asked Mary. "Not here in the cold?"

"We will make our home under the stars, my girl. This campsite will feel as warm and friendly as your tree house in the Upper Kingdom in a day or two." Pops pulled tent stakes out of his pack.

"But I thought we were here to build tree houses," said Bobby.

"That we are, my boy," said Pops. "But a tree house is first built *here*." He pointed to his chest. Then he bent back over and started pulling more tools and supplies out of his pack, humming as he went. Bobby was baffled, but said no more.

Tommy kicked a rock. "So we're just going to live outside and—"

"—learn to trust each other," said Pops.

"But what about wild animals?" asked Mary. "And what about . . . other things? Are there any people living in this part of the forest, Pops? Bad people?"

"Bad *people*? You mean like bandits and such? Ah, yes, you are remembering the story I told a few days ago. Hmm . . . I wouldn't worry much about bandits. Like I always say, 'The less you have, the less you have to lose.' Besides, we can't let a few mountain cats or thieves frighten us too much." He pulled a cooking pot from his pack. "We will see creatures much more frightening than those, I'm afraid. This is a time to learn of courage and trust, not fear and worry." Mary smiled weakly and tried not to look too nervous.

"Sounds great!" said Bobby, pumping his fists. "I've always wondered what it might be like to live in the Great Forest. This will be the best adventure we've ever had!" He picked up the cooking pot. "Pops, we can put our campfire over here, and I'll go find some wood before dinner, if—"

"Bobby!" Pops took the pot back. "Bobby, this is very exciting for you, and I do believe you will have quite a remarkable time. However, there is one thing you must never forget, as long as you live." Pops pulled Tommy and Mary close to Bobby. "All of you, never lose this thought: this is not the Great Forest. This is the Lesser Forest. This is nothing like the Upper Kingdom. Do not be deceived by apparent similarities."

Confused, Bobby looked at Tommy. Then he looked all around. "But it seems the same to me. It has the same trees and sounds and smells. What is so different?"

"Is something wrong, Pops?" asked Tommy.

Pops took a few steps back. "Children, this is very serious . . . this mission we are on. In fact, I would have to say that the lives of many people depend on the things we will do and the plans we will make. Our mission is bigger than building one tree house. Our enemy is on the move, though we do not yet know his plans against us. But you must each know that you will be taken prisoner by the enemy if you ever lose sight of the fact that you are intruders into his kingdom. Look around you."

All three children looked at the ground.

"Go on, look around you," said Pops. "All of you."

Tommy lifted his head and looked throughout the dimly lit forest in every direction. Bobby and Mary did the same.

"Everything you see is under his control," said Pops. "The trees, the animals, the hills—they all are the claimed territory of the Dark Prince of the Lower Kingdom. Simply by standing on this insignificant hill in this seemingly unpopulated area, we have declared war against him. We are uninvited, unwelcome trespassers in this land."

Pops paced back and forth in front of the line of rocks as he talked. "We are on a special mission from our King, and for our mission to be a success we must depend upon the strength that comes from his kingdom and on the wisdom that flows from the River. We must never become so shortsighted as to think that we belong in this backward place. The moment this kingdom feels like our home is the moment we surrender our mission, and our hearts, to the evil prince."

Mary slipped her hand into Tommy's.

"Pops," said Tommy. "I'm sorry. We didn't mean to seem careless.

It's just that, well, the Tree House Village, and here in the forest, it doesn't feel like the Lower Kingdom at all. I will never forget when I passed through the gate with the Prince the first time. The Lower Kingdom was so scary and dirty, so noisy and wrong, and . . . well, it was evil. But this trip, this time, has been easy, almost fun." Tommy tugged on the long sleeves of his jacket. "I mean, the last time I was here I even looked different—though I'm not sure how. But I was accepted as one of them—like a grown-up. That hasn't happened to us at all. It just doesn't feel like we are actually in the Lower Kingdom."

Mary and Bobby nodded and Tommy continued. "The tree houses by the River seem just like the ones in the Great Forest— maybe better. Roger is so pleasant and friendly that though he looks old, I can sense nothing about him that would not belong in the Upper Kingdom. And, forgive me if this is terrible, but I would almost say that I actually prefer the excitement of the Tree House Village on the banks of the River to my life in the Upper Kingdom." He paused. "Is that wrong of me, Pops?"

Pops looked up into the nearly dark sky. "No, Tommy. It doesn't surprise me at all that you like the Tree House Village or the River . . . and I wouldn't say that what you are feeling is wrong. I can remember falling in love with this place the first time I crawled out of the River. This land once belonged to the Great King, you know, before Senkrad's rebellion. The entire Lower Kingdom once belonged to him. That's why it looks and feels so beautiful at times. The truth of his greatness is here. But the Lower Kingdom is no longer his . . . not entirely. It has been stolen and tainted."

Pops stepped closer to Tommy and met his eyes. "Tommy, you are somewhat correct when you say that this isn't the Lower Kingdom. The truth is, this is what we tree-house builders call Middleland. It is part of the Lower Kingdom, but the River has changed it. The tree houses themselves have changed it. A genuine tree house is a little taste—an embassy of the Upper Kingdom here in the lower one."

Pops looked up to see three sets of eyes piercing his. After all the hours of teaching, he knew the words that would stand out would be those he spoke this night. "Tommy," he continued, "the farther away from the River we go, the worse it will get. The Gate of Separation is just over that hill to the east, about a four-hour hike from here. We have already moved into greater danger by being this far away from the River, though I am confident we are safe to camp here tonight."

"Where will we build our tree house, Pops?" Mary's fear had turned to curiosity.

Pops smiled. "I don't yet know. Farther out than this, I'm sure. The Prince will visit us soon. Then he will tell us where to build."

"Does the Prince decide where all of the tree houses are built?" asked Tommy.

"He used to. Most tree-house builders do not bother asking anymore. That's why so many houses are along the River and so few toward the city. They are harder to build toward the city, but lately that is where the Prince has been directing us to start new ones."

"How many tree houses are there in the Lower Kingdom, Pops?" Bobby asked.

"Hmm . . ." Pops counted in his head. "At least a hundred by now. It's hard to know for sure because new ones appear every so often and old ones are sometimes destroyed by Senkrad's army. Or . . . abandoned."

"And how many are in the village—along the bank of the River?" Tommy asked.

Pops winced. "Most of them, I am sorry to say." He sighed. "The Prince directed us to build the first ten tree houses along the bank of the River. Then he asked me to lead the building of one just a few hundred yards into the forest. When I told the others, they refused to help me. They said that the Prince had already put his strategy into action and that it would be unwise for me to go against his wishes. They also said that the first round of houses were not yet fully operational and must be completed before we could even think about building more. They even threatened to burn down any tree houses not built within fifty yards of the River."

"Why didn't the Prince tell them what he told you?" Mary asked.

"He did. But they couldn't hear him. None of them would enter the River anymore because they had grown consumed with their work. Without time in the River, deception can overpower the best of us. Before long, the prince of the Lower Kingdom had deceived everyone so thoroughly that they actually mistook his voice for the voice of the Good Prince."

"What has become of those people?" asked Tommy.

"Many were taken prisoner." Pops looked away and covered his eyes for a moment with his hand. "I'm sorry. They were my friends, and it's hard to talk about sometimes. Forgive me." He exhaled. "A few of them, the most deceived of all, were allowed to stay here and disrupt the work. They are the ones who argue with one another and continue to build tree houses along the River."

"Is Roger one of them?" asked Mary.

"Oh goodness, no!" Pops's face brightened. "Roger is like a brother to me. There are others like him too. The River is uniting a new breed of builders who will listen to the voice of the Prince and serve together in unity."

The children were quiet. Then Bobby climbed on top of a rock near him and stood there, balancing. "So that is what we are?" he said. "We are the new breed of builders?"

The thought clearly pleased Pops. "Yes . . . you are indeed, Bobby. You are the new breed. And you must carry on what you learn here. That a real tree house comes not from plans on paper, or certain shapes of wood, or the designs of men and women. Nor is its worth defined by its location, its size, or its age. A real tree house is built in the hearts of people who love each other enough to make something together. And its value comes from the working together, and what that brings to all those who come to it, see it, or hear of it. Working together is never as easy as working alone. But it is always better."

"Pops looked around at the looming darkness. "Now, my new breed, it is time to make camp before we cannot see a thing."

Under Pops's direction, the children started a fire, put up the large tent, and cooked the evening meal. Afterward they all talked and laughed inside the tent, telling stories. Before long, the children fell asleep, but Pops stared at the canvas above him. He wanted to rest and he knew he needed to trust, but . . .

Frustrated, he crawled from the tent to check on the fire. Hadn't he covered the embers? What was that golden glow?

"What in the—" Pops covered his mouth with both hands.

Five female messengers, each at least six feet tall, stood around the tent, swords drawn. They faced outward, their eyes focused on the forest all around. One looked over her shoulder at Pops, bowed her head slightly, and then returned to her guard stance.

Pops stared, taking in their glory as best he could. Though they stood quite still, they had a musical quality about them—as if an orchestra were playing in the far, far distance. Then, with a great sense of peace and calm, Pops returned to the tent with heavy eyes and fell asleep. His King was doing something new in the Lower Kingdom.

The Final Warning

Pops made it his practice to visit the River every morning of his life. When he was far away from her, he visited her by walking off to a quiet, lonely place and imagining himself in her waters. Early in the morning he walked the perimeter of the campsite while the children slept. Pops knew this morning was special.

Pops packed his knapsack quietly so as not to wake the children. They needed as much sleep as they could get during these peaceful days. He scratched out a note on a scrap of paper that he found in the pocket of his coat:

> *Tommy,*
> *Take Mary and Bobby to the River today.*
> *I will meet you back here for supper.*
> *Pops*

Pops gently placed the note on Tommy's chest and walked eastward through the forest toward a large green hill in the distance. He closed his eyes and let the River push and pull him toward the hill.

He remembered his first few adventures in the Lower Kingdom, how frightened and worried he became when left alone in the forest or in the city. He thought about the first time he could feel the flow of the River without actually being in her waters. How easy it was for him to submit to her now.

Before he knew it, the flow of the River came to an abrupt halt. He opened his eyes to find himself at the very top of the hill and sat down on an old tree stump, facing the city below. Piercing through the thick brown fog settled over the city, the Palace of the Dark Prince glistened in the sunlight like a jewel. "It is made of trash and mud," he said aloud, as if to remind himself.

"Indeed it is, my friend."

"Prince!" Pops turned and immediately appeared as a seven-year-old boy with freckles and black fuzzy hair.

"Freddie, it is good to see you." The Prince hugged the little boy and sat down with him in the grass. "How are the others doing?"

"They are well, Prince. They still have much to learn before we will be ready to build the tree house, but they are very promising recruits. I am considering extending the training by a week, as we have not yet even explored their gifts."

"Does Tommy wear his jacket?"

"He does. But it is just so big on him. Sometimes it seems to weigh him down."

"He hasn't adjusted to his Lower Kingdom status yet?"

"No, Prince," Pops replied. "None of the children have." Of course, transformation had always been a mystery to him. He wondered aloud, "Should I have done something more to bring their transformation about?"

"No, I'm sure they will transform soon." The Prince stroked his beard. "Are they fully aware that they are in the Lower Kingdom?"

"They were confused at first. They seem to have a full understanding now."

"Very good. That will help."

Pops laid back on the grass, glad to be in the presence of the Prince. They spoke of things good and bad, including the state of the Tree House Village and the ongoing corruption spreading throughout the King's children there. The boy's voice squeaked with excitement when speaking of his plans, but then lowered in anger when he described the various deceptions and distractions created by certain residents of the village. After a while, the two stood up, and Freddie appeared as the old builder once again.

"What you have told me disturbs me, my child, but I have news that is far more troubling." The Prince's eyes grew sad and he put his arm around the man's shoulders as the two walked to the far edge of the hill.

"Tell me." Pops felt safe with the Prince, and safe with any news he might bring.

"The messengers have informed me that the Dark Prince is now capable of creating the great disruption he has longed for. He's moving forward on his plans to spread what he calls the Long Night."

"What is that?"

"A project he has been secretly planning since his defeat at Senkrad's Hill. You know his greatest successes have come through his sly deceptions. He now plans to deceive the entire Lower Kingdom by darkening their vision. He has been experimenting with ways of doing this for some time." The Prince stopped and stared out at the view of the city, such as it was. "In fact, I recently was in one of the deep rooms of his palace, and saw the fruit of one such experiment. But that is no matter now. This plan is bigger. As big as the sky."

Pops shivered as a breeze chilled his spine. "The sky?"

"He has been working, or rather, he has been forcing his servants to work to create a facility in which a fire can be built. An enormous fire. That facility has been finished for some weeks. And now he is gathering his fuel of choice—wood. The trees."

Pops looked fearful. "The trees? But I don't understand. You mean, he wants all of them?"

"He needs them to burn, together with some evil compound he has developed, to produce a kind of smoke. Have you been to the city at all lately, my friend?" Pops shook his head. "Ah, well, if you had, you would have noticed it. The air is harder to breathe. The sky seems more polluted, yet the factories have not increased. It is this smoke of the Dark Prince. He has been releasing it in small amounts, testing its potency."

"So this smoke, it will make the sky cloudy, like it gets over the city? But what good can that do for him? I mean, it is dismal, but certainly people can just get used to that."

"This smoke will not just cloud the sky, it will obscure the sun! Its blackness will be as complete as that of the heart of its master, blotting out every ray, every glimmer, every star. Day will appear as night throughout the entire Lower Kingdom, including Middleland and the Gate." The Prince turned his back on the sight of the Palace of the Dark Prince. He bowed his head, and uttered some words. Pops was used to this. It was the way of the Prince to talk with his father. The Great King could hear the Prince's voice no matter where he was in either kingdom.

When the Prince had been silent for some moments, Pops asked, "But I don't understand. The darkness will make life difficult, to be sure, but what is that to the Prince? Where is the deception?"

"You said it earlier, Pops. 'People can just get used to that.' That's what he wants. He wants the inhabitants of the Lower Kingdom to learn to live in utter darkness and no longer be able to find access to my father's kingdom. He wants them to get used to the darkness." The Prince squatted on the ground and watched some ants crawl to their hill and descend into their underground home. "Do you know what happens to creatures that live in the dark, Pops?"

"Like cave animals, you mean? They live in utter darkness, so they have no need for sight, as we know it. They are blind."

"Now you see. Yes, they are blind. And if an animal who once lived in light is made to live in darkness, it not only loses its sight—it grows to fear the light. To hate the light. To run away from the light." The Prince rose and surveyed his friend's face. How much he hated frightening the children of the King!

"I know this news is unsettling, my friend, and it gets worse yet. But you must know these things. And you must not forget that I will always be with you." Pops swallowed the lump that had been in his throat. The Prince continued, "This darkness will give the prince control of the Lower Kingdom. He alone will control the light. He will control the people's fear. But there is more to his project than mere darkness, I am afraid."

"What could be worse than an eternal night?"

The Prince placed his hands on Pops's shoulders. "He is planning on destroying the tree houses. All of them." Pops gasped. The Prince went on, with a grim expression, "On the second day of darkness, he will order his Phantom Messengers to destroy all the tree houses in his kingdom to use for fuel in the furnace of his palace. This will help him to produce the smoke needed for his Long Night. And it will throw the people into utter confusion. He will arrest or kill all those who oppose the Phantom Messengers."

"This is too terrible to comprehend," said Pops. "The Phantom Messengers—I have heard of them, but that is all. Where do they come from? What are their powers? How do we fight them?"

"The children are not the only ones who have the choice to follow the Dark Prince. Messengers of the King may choose this path as well. But when they do, they change. They become dark and evil creatures, quite intimidating to say the least . . . but they are not invincible. If you choose to stay, I will send you someone who will show you how to defeat them."

"If I choose? I am already here. Where would I go?" Pops was a little hurt. Did the Prince not have faith in him? Of course, he had been scared and shocked by this news, but he had no intention of giving up. Did the Prince think he was too old for such a fight?

"Pops, I want to give you the choice to come back to the Upper Kingdom. This is not exactly what you thought you were signing on for. This battle will be terrible. I must know that you have chosen this assignment yourself. You must know that you have chosen it, or else you will surely doubt yourself in the days to come." The Prince looked intensely at Pops.

"My Prince and my friend, you have never led me astray. Why would I doubt you now? This task will be my last and greatest. It will be my honor and your glory. I will fight to the very death if I must."

"Very well. And know this, my friend. If you die, it will not be the end for you. Never will you cease to exist. That mask of an old man you wear around this place may end up ruined and useless, but you will never be extinguished from my father's Kingdom. You are a child of the King, forever seven years old. Do you understand?"

"I do, my Prince. Now more than ever."

"You will need to explain all of this to Tommy and the others. If anyone wants to return to my father's palace, you must deliver him or her through the gate by nightfall tomorrow. I believe that the Long Night will begin sometime the day after tomorrow. There are others here not unlike you, children of the King, who are working a plan to delay the evil project even as we speak. But you must know that their best effort will only buy us a few hours. After the black smoke spews from the palace, no one will be able to find the door to enter the Upper Kingdom. And my father will not allow his children in the passage to the Lower Kingdom through the River or the gate until the Long Night has ended. All access at every level will be denied. Only I will be allowed to pass through, and even I will not be allowed to enter unless my father sends me."

"What of my new recruits?" asked Pops. "They aren't ready for this yet. They haven't even begun phase two of training. We just set up camp last night."

"They are as ready as they will be," said the Prince. "They will learn as they go."

"And what of those residents of the Lower Kingdom who accept the invitation while passage is restricted? Will they be allowed through the gate?"

"You must take them into the River and tell them to stay there until they see light from the sun again. The River will slow their aging and protect them until the Long Night ends. Get anyone you can into the River at any cost."

Pops had so many questions regarding the future that he could not think of what to ask next.

"The River will guide you, Pops. Feel her as she tugs you to the right or left. Listen to her song. Teach the others to feel her and listen to her as well."

"And what of the tree house you sent us here to build . . . where shall we build it?" asked Pops.

"You will know when the time comes. Remember that not all tree houses have to be built in trees, and not all have to resemble houses. You must learn what it means to build as you go. Build on the run. Build in battle and in times of peace. Build every day with whatever resources you have around you. This will be your key to victory. Build your next house in the city and build it without wood or hammer or nails."

One last question nagged at Pops. "Forgive me, my Prince, but surely you are powerful enough to lead an army of messengers down this hill to destroy that trash-heap palace before sundown. Why do you need me to help? Why not spare us all the battle?"

The Prince said nothing, but stared down at the Dark Prince's palace as if tempted to destroy it. "You will understand fully on the other side," he said finally. "When we meet in the Palace of the Great King for breakfast on your first day of retirement, I will look you in the eyes and you will say, 'Now I see.' Until then you must trust and fight for what is right. There is no peace without a fight."

Pops bear-hugged the Prince. "That I can do. I can trust, and with what little I have got left in these bones, I can fight. I must go now and tell the others."

"Yes, you need to hurry. And I must talk to a few others in the valley. Be strong and be wise, Pops. I am counting on you."

"And I am honored, my Prince." Pops bowed low.

"I'll see you on the other side, then." The Prince broke into a jog down the eastern slope of the hill. "Remember!" he yelled over his shoulder. "Wait for the one I am sending to help you!"

Pops turned westward without saying good-bye. With his eyes closed, he hurdled stones and ducked under tree limbs as the River pulled him back to the training camp, where he sat down to wait for the children's return.

Transformations

"Pops! Pops!" Mary's terrified screams echoed through the forest. "Pops! I can't find you! Where are you?"

Mary burst through the clearing and ran toward the campfire. Big tears ran down her cheeks and she struggled to breathe. "Tommy . . . he . . . it's . . . ." She buried her head in the old man's chest.

"Mary! Where's Tommy?" His voice shook.

"He's old! He has changed into an old person. He has been taken over by the evil prince. And Bobby too—they are both *old*!"

"When?"

"Just now. I mean, not long ago." She wiped her tears and tried to compose herself. "We were all swimming in the River with Roger, and Tommy started to—to change."

Pops began to laugh. "My sweet Mary." He knelt down and wiped her tears with the sleeve of his jacket. "Tommy hasn't grown old; he has transformed."

"What do you mean?" Mary looked up at him, hurt and confused by his laughter.

"Only his body looks old. He is still seven, just like you and me."

Mary looked at Pops with a curious expression. She remembered when Tommy had asked her to be a part of his team that he had said Pops was seven, though he looked older. But that seemed so long ago, and she had become used to being with the old man. It seemed impossible to see him any other way.

Pops seemed to read her mind. Only Tommy had ever seen him as Freddie, on the day they met in the Upper Kingdom. "Mary, close your eyes for a moment."

Pops transformed into Freddie. This particular transformation came from a power outside himself, and Pops was grateful for it. "Open now."

Mary knew it was Pops who spoke, yet his voice had never been quite so innocent and squeaky. She opened her eyes to see a little black-haired boy. The body was that of a child, but the eyes were unmistakably those of her teacher, mentor, and friend. She could see the truth in the transformation.

She extended her hand to the little boy. "My name is Mary. What is yours?" She smiled at the thought of Pops as a child.

"My name is Freddie. Some of my friends call me Pops."

They both laughed.

But then Mary's voice became strange. "Pops, I don't feel . . . right." A mysterious tingling, unlike anything she had ever felt before, confused and terrified her.

"Just let it happen, Mary." Pops immediately reappeared as the old builder. "Just let it happen. Just submit."

Mary closed her eyes and rapidly transformed into a tall, confident young woman, perhaps thirty years old, with long, brown, wavy hair and a face more beautiful than a sunrise. It was no surprise to Pops that a person as sweet as Mary would appear so lovely. He smiled and laughed as he watched her spirit reflect in a physical masterpiece.

Mary allowed the transformation to complete before she opened her eyes and looked at Pops. It felt odd to look at her teacher without tilting her head up. "Pops, your face! Is it that terrible?" Her mature voice startled her.

"Oh goodness, no." Pops wiped his eyes. "You are the most beautiful creature in the Lower Kingdom. You are a lovely, lovely woman. Look at yourself in the mirror of your locket."

Mary's eyes lit up and she blushed as she looked at her reflection. "I want to find Tommy."

"I'd guess he wants to see you too." Pops grabbed the knapsack at his side. "Let's go back to the River." He offered his arm.

"Where were you today, Pops? You were gone such a long time."

"I had to meet the Prince."

Mary wondered at the somber tone of his voice when he said those words, but she didn't feel afraid. She set her face toward the River, enjoying her new longer stride. Something more than her body had changed. She was ready for whatever was about to happen.

Most of the village tree houses were closed and darkened for the night, but outside Roger's tree house four men stood in a circle, talking.

"They haven't noticed us yet, Pops," said Mary. "Tommy's on the left, and Bobby is talking to Roger."

"Who is the other young man?" Pops asked.

"I don't know. He wasn't here when I left. Do you think he is friendly?"

"I assume he's a friend of Roger's." Pops raised his voice, risking waking up the entire village. "Roger! Have you new friends to introduce to me?"

"I have three new friends!" Roger called. "Where are you?"

Pops and Mary moved into the light of the lantern hanging from Roger's tree house.

"Pops, you're getting too old to have girlfriends. Who is this beautiful young lady?"

"Oh, stop," said Pops. "You are embarrassing her." He reached out his hand to Tommy. "Name's Freddie, my friends call me Pops." Tommy's coat fit him well.

"Pops, it's me, Tommy!"

"Of course it's you! Do you think I'm blind?" Pops hugged Tommy and pretended to try to pick him up. "You are a horse of a man! And not all that bad looking." Tommy was well-built and handsome, in his late twenties. Pops grinned. Something about the way Tommy held himself gave a good feeling to those around him. Like they were standing in the shelter of a tall, strong tree.

"Hello, Pops." Bobby appeared a bit older and a bit shorter than Tommy, with brown skin and a full black beard. He extended a strong hand. His voice was deep, and he had the eyes of a lion . . . and biceps to match.

Bobby smiled at Mary. "I'm Bobby. And you are?" He spoke politely, extending his hand.

Mary smiled. "I'm Mary."

Bobby gasped. Tommy grabbed Mary around the waist and hugged her, swinging her legs in a full circle before returning her to the ground.

"Mary, you are—"

"Beautiful? Yes, she is, Tommy. Remember, though, outer beauty can be both good and bad. Love and respect are based on the Mary we have always known."

Tommy grinned at Pops, understanding, but still mesmerized by Mary's transformation.

Pops raised his eyebrows at the stranger in the group, standing next to Bobby. Thin, in his mid-thirties, he wore a plain business suit, white shirt, and thick black-rimmed glasses. His blond hair and his clothes were damp. "This man claims that the Prince asked him to join us," Bobby said. "He came out of the River less than an hour ago."

"It's an honor to meet you, Pops. My name is Luke. I have come as a representative of the Prince. I am very informed in matters of the Lower Kingdom, and I am here to serve your team in any way that might prove helpful."

Pops shook Luke's hand. "You are the one the Prince promised," he said. "It is good to have you aboard."

"Luke and I have been on a mission once before," said Tommy.

"Yes." Luke removed his glasses and rubbed his eyes. "It was a dark time for me. I was deceived and arrogant and thus was taken captive by the enemy. Though I regret my choices, I also now see the good that has come out of what happened to me. I feel as though I have seen evil from the inside out. This is my first mission since that awful day. I submit myself to your leadership, Pops."

"You have really changed, Luke," said Tommy.

Luke smiled. "For the better, I hope. I have spent all of my time since that day in the Upper Kingdom with the Prince and the King. I know that I am not who I once was, but I am still not sure who I am becoming." He put his glasses back on. "The Prince has sent me to teach you how to fight against our enemy. I am sure that Pops has informed you about the coming of the Long Night."

Tommy, Mary, Bobby, and Roger all turned toward Pops, faces confused.

"Luke, I have not yet," said Pops. "I have just returned from my meeting with the Prince. Perhaps now would be a good time to discuss things. Roger, how about some tea?"

The Decision

Everything about Roger's small tree house welcomed visitors into a state of peace and simplicity. Three wooden rocking chairs sat in the main room, along with a few throw rugs. A small fireplace in the far corner provided a cheerful place for heating water for tea. Roger tended the fire as his guests crowded together and made themselves comfortable.

Pops lowered himself into one of the rocking chairs and considered the conversation about to take place. Mary and Bobby sat in the other two chairs, and Tommy stood near the fireplace. Luke leaned against the doorway at the entrance to the room, his hands deep in his pockets.

Tommy spoke first. "Tell us, Pops, what is this all about? Why has Luke come?"

Pops felt everyone's eyes on him. "The Prince came to see me today. I met him several miles east of here."

"In the city?" asked Bobby.

"No. Nearby."

"Did he tell you about this Long Night Luke spoke of?" Mary always liked to get to the point.

"That he did," said Pops. "He gave me all of the unfortunate details. And now, I am afraid, I must share them with you. The Prince—"

The teakettle shrieked and everyone jumped. "Perhaps we will wait to share tea until you have finished speaking, Pops." Roger placed the teakettle away from the fire with a shaky hand.

"Very well." Pops took a deep breath. "The Dark Prince has been hard at work on a secret project for many years. Our Good Prince has been made aware of the horrible truth that the scheme now stands on the verge of completion. Alas, we are days, maybe hours, away from this evil coming upon us all."

"This Long Night is the project that you speak of?" Roger asked.

Pops sat back in his rocker. "Yes, my friend. Senkrad has figured out a way to fill the entire valley with a dense smoke, blocking the light from above. The Prince says it will be so terrible and dark that every person here will be blinded. Senkrad's scheme is that the people will grow used to the darkness, and fear any natural light. Once that happens, he will have control of the people."

"Why would he do such a terrible thing?" Mary asked.

"The Dark Prince is motivated by fear and hatred. He is afraid that all his subjects will discover the Upper Kingdom and leave him utterly alone. And he hates the Upper Kingdom, and anything that reflects its glory. He would rather have blind subjects, cowering in his charge, than people who are free to make their own way, and thus, choose their own way in this world."

"We should just go back home and get help," said Tommy. "Then we could destroy his palace before the smoke starts to rise."

Pops shook his head. "There isn't time for that, Tommy. If anything is to happen to thwart this evil plan, it is up to us to see it through. There is one thing more—"

"A good thing, I hope," said Roger.

"No Roger, quite the opposite . . . a very hideous thing.

Mary's fingers started twisting the ends of her hair. "What is it, Pops? You can tell us. We must know everything if we are going to be able to help the Prince."

"A group of messengers have aligned themselves with Senkrad. They are called Phantom Messengers. They are vile creatures. These Phantoms will be released shortly after the Long Night begins, with strict orders . . ." Pops looked at Roger. "With strict orders to destroy the tree houses—all of them, even those here inside the Tree House Village."

Roger's head sank into his hands. Tommy went to him and placed his arm around the man.

"Phantom means 'pretend,' you know," said Luke. "They are a serious threat and quite terrifying, don't get me wrong. But they are pretenders. They will be revealed for what they are. That is why I am here. I will help you defeat the Phantom Messengers—the Prince says it is what I was born to do."

Tommy glanced across the room at Mary.

"Thank you, Luke," Pops said. "I trust that you will be a great help to us all. There is one other thing that must be said tonight. The King will block travel to and from the Lower Kingdom once the Long Night begins. No one will be allowed to access the Lower Kingdom, either by the River or the Gate, and no one in the Lower Kingdom may return to the Upper Kingdom until the Long Night is over."

"He's right," said Luke. "I was the last to leave. No one else is coming out."

"So we are trapped here, for . . . ever?" Mary's newfound courage began to waver a bit.

Tommy spoke, his arm still around Roger. "Not forever, Mary. We are just stationed here by the Prince until the Long Night is over. And then we will all get to go home, right, Pops?"

"Yes, in one way or another. But no one should remain here against his or her will. Anyone who wants to leave may do so tomorrow. I will personally escort you to the Gate of Separation first thing in the morning." Pops sighed. "So . . . now is the time to let me know. Either way—no judgment from me, but are you in or out?"

Luke's crisp voice cut through the tense air. "Obviously, I'm in. It's what I do. It's why I am here. I will not think less of anyone who wants to go back, since the rest of you came without knowing the full scope of this mission."

Silence again.

"I am in as well." Tommy looked at Luke and then at Mary. "It's what I was born to do."

Mary was solemn and spoke deliberately. "I'm in as well—I was born to help him."

"How could I turn down an adventure like this?" said Bobby. "I'm in. Let's do this."

Pops's steady gaze rested on Roger. "This is my last one, old friend. I'd love to end it with you . . ."

Roger shook. He was the only one of the children who could see the full implication of this commitment. "It's just a mask, right, Freddie?"

"It's just a mask, Roger, just like mine . . . "

Roger pulled Pops out of his chair and hugged him. Then he whispered just loud enough for everyone to hear, "I'm in, Freddie. Of course, I'm in."

The Last Breakfast

Tommy awoke the next morning to the familiar shriek of Roger's teakettle. Mary and Bobby were still asleep on the rugs near the fireplace. He yawned. Where were the others?

"Morning, Tommy." Roger came into the room with a bundle of papers. "Pops and Luke are just outside, at the pier. They want you to join them, and they need these." He put the papers down on a small table. "It seems like we have some quick decisions to make. But, have some tea first?"

"No thanks. Has more happened since last night?" He was eager to get outside.

"I can't say for sure. I will wake your friends and send them to you shortly. Take the papers now and go. And Tommy, your coat. You should be wearing it from now on, without exception."

"Oh . . . of course." He slid his arms into the patched sleeves. *Humility*. The coat fit perfectly, like he was supposed to have worn it his whole life.

"You look exactly like Pops when he was younger," said Roger.

Outside the tree house, Tommy viewed the overcast sky. When had the weather turned so cold? He buttoned his jacket and thrust his hands into the pockets, with the bundle of papers under his arm, and walked the short distance to the River.

Tiny snowflakes gently floated in the cool breeze. He caught one on his tongue and spat at once on the ground. It was not snow at all, but some sort of ash from a fire.

"Over here, Tommy!" Pops yelled.

Luke motioned to the papers under Tommy's arm. "Are those the maps?"

"I haven't looked at them yet." He handed the bundle to Luke.

"It's started, Tommy," said Pops. "White ash is falling all over the Lower Kingdom. It must be much worse than this closer to the palace. We need to make our plans right now. No more time to delay."

"Seems to me somebody has to go straight to the heart of the problem," said Tommy. "What if Bobby and I go into the city and destroy the furnace in the palace?"

Luke looked up from the maps and peered over the top of his glasses. "How are you going to do that?"

"I don't know."

"I was sure hoping you did," said Luke.

"I hadn't thought about dividing up," said Pops. "We could do that. You and Bobby could head to the city while Luke and Mary and I stay here to guard the tree houses in the village."

Luke spread out one of the maps on a large wooden post of the pier. "I don't know what to do about the furnace, but I think I know how to stop the Phantoms, or at least slow them down. At a minimum, I could protect the village with the help of a few others."

"What of the other tree houses, outside the village?" asked Pops.

"They are vulnerable. We could send Tommy and Bobby on a less direct route into the city." Luke fumbled through the maps and unfolded one that showed the layout of the entire Lower Kingdom. He studied it for a minute, then said, "Here. If they took this route, they could warn all of these tree houses on their way to the lower palace. Hopefully all of them, anyway. It might be too late for some. No doubt the Phantoms are already on the move."

Tommy moved over to inspect the map. "So the red dots represent tree houses?"

"Not necessarily," Pops warned. He scratched his chin under his beard. "The red dots are buildings that look like tree houses. They may or may not contain children of the King. It's a tricky thing to figure out. There are also, no doubt, some tree houses that have sprung up since the map was created. They sometimes have a way of just . . . appearing."

"But how will we know who to warn?" asked Tommy. "How will we know who to trust?"

"I'll send Roger with you. He will know," said Pops. "I trust him more than myself in these matters. But regardless of who lives in these houses, the residents should be warned."

"These Phantoms will obey their orders to destroy any tree house they see," Luke said. "They are soldiers. Blind obedience to Senkrad's orders is all they know. My advice would be to warn everyone, but trust no one."

Pops walked to the edge of the pier and faced them. "Well, I guess that's our plan. May the River guide us all." Closing his eyes, he fell backward into the water with a huge splash.

Luke looked at Tommy, a little confused.

"He's really, really into the River," said Tommy.

"Oh. Well then, why not?" Luke readied himself for a dive.

"Why not indeed!" Tommy said with a grin. "Race you!" Luke and Tommy took off in a dead sprint down the pier and dove headfirst into the River.

A cry came from the direction of Roger's tree house. "Wait for us!" Bobby and Mary hurried down the pier and jumped into the water.

The River, normally cool, felt warm and soothing that morning, as if the King himself were breathing warmth into the waters of the mountain to comfort his children before they went into battle on his behalf in a dark, strange world.

After about a half hour had passed, they heard Roger calling. "Breakfast! Everyone, come and eat!"

Pops exited the River after the others. He hated leaving her waters. Atop the pier, he shook his body like a wet dog and wrung the water from his beard. The dark sky was unlike anything he had ever seen in all his travels. Midmorning looked like dusk.

Roger poked his head through the small window in his kitchen. "C'mon, you wet old man! Eggs don't stay warm forever! We are all waiting for you!" Roger loved breakfast more than any meal of the day, and he was determined to have one last normal breakfast before what he imagined would be a terrible battle with the approaching evil horde.

"We should eat fast and then get about our business," said Luke. His plate was heavy with scrambled eggs and strawberries.

Pops stayed in the doorway.

"What's wrong, Pops?" Mary motioned to the empty chair at the table. "You should try to eat something."

"This may be our last breakfast together for quite some time," said Pops. "I just want to remember it. This very memory, what you are seeing in this moment, may be all that will get you through what is to come."

"Then eat what I've fixed for you," said Roger. He set a platter of pancakes on the table. "Sit down and eat with us."

"Wait, I have something for all of you first." Pops rummaged through his knapsack and brought a napkin-wrapped bundle to the table.

"What is it, Pops?" asked Tommy.

"*Shh*. You'll see." Pops unfolded the napkins.

Roger inhaled.

"Is that——?" asked Mary.

"Those are . . . I mean . . ." Bobby stumbled.

"Cookies from the King's palace," said Tommy.

"That's right. I've carried them with me for many years. It's time they were eaten."

"I haven't seen one in so long, Freddie." Roger's voice cracked. "How many do you have?"

"A dozen," said Pops. "Two for each of us. One for now and one for the next time we are together again. All of you, take one."

"Are they still good?" asked Mary. "You've been carrying them around for years?"

"A cookie from the King's palace never goes bad," said Luke.

"To the King and our Prince," Pops whispered. He raised his cookie as if it were a goblet from the King's banquet table, and the others did the same.

"To the King and our Prince."

Pops waited to be the last to taste his cookie. He wanted to see the others experience theirs first. They all closed their eyes and took their first bite. Mary began to giggle. Roger began to cry. Then Pops took a bite, and everyone at the table transformed into seven-year-old children again.

"Roger? Are you OK?" asked Bobby. "

Pops answered for him. "He's remembering. He hasn't been back to the Upper Kingdom for a long, long time."

"I almost forgot what they tasted like," said Roger through his tears. "I've almost forgotten everything. I can barely remember what it's like."

"But you didn't forget," Pops said. "That's the important thing. You'll be home soon." Pops hugged his old friend.

As they finished eating their cookies, each one began transforming back into a grown-up state. Luke was the first to change, and then Bobby.

"I can't wait to get home again and play hide-and-seek in the gardens," Tommy confessed to Mary.

"I know. Me too. I'll see you again when we get there." Mary winked and tossed the last morsel of her cookie in her mouth at the same time Tommy finished his.

Roger composed himself enough to finish his cookie with Pops.

Pops returned to his seat and passed out the last six cookies. "Keep these with you and don't lose them. We won't eat these again until we all eat them together upon our return to the Upper Kingdom. That is my promise to you."

"To our first breakfast together in the Upper Kingdom!" Tommy raised his cup of tea as a toast.

Separation

Tommy stood outside of Roger's tree house with his coat buttoned to his neck and a knapsack slung over his right shoulder. He methodically made markings with a red pen all over the map of the Lower Kingdom that Luke had given him earlier. Bobby sat on the ground a few feet away. He double-checked the inventory in his bag, which included a hunting knife, a torch, and a change of clothes.

"It's getting worse," said Bobby. "Should be the brightest part of the day, but it's darker than it was an hour ago."

"I know . . . it's eerie," said Tommy. "Once Roger is ready we can leave. We have a long hike today. We should move eastward through the Lesser Forest to warn the first tree houses outside the village." Tommy bent down to show Bobby the map as he circled one of the red dots with his pen. Someone had written MAGUS above the dot.

"What does *Magus* mean?" asked Bobby.

"I'm not sure, Bobby. I didn't write that," said Tommy. "We can ask Roger on the way if he'll just hurry—"

A massive boom followed by a cracking sound came from deep within the forest.

"What was that? Was that thunder?" asked Luke.

Tommy stared deeply into the darkening forest behind the row of tree houses. "I don't think so. Sounded like a tree falling . . . or being cut down. We should go now," he said. He folded the map and shoved it into one of the many pockets in his patched jacket.

Just then Roger emerged from his home with Pops. Luke and Mary trailed behind him. "And remember to water the plants in the kitchen window, Mary . . . not that it matters much I suppose with this dreaded darkness. Pops, there are extra blankets in the storage area above the bed—"

"Roger!" Pops snapped. "We will be fine. Your house will be fine. Now you must go. Help the boys warn the others."

Roger breathed deeply and looked at his old friend. He then looked at Luke and Mary. "Of course. It is only a house after all. You three be careful and help those here in the village." He looked back to Tommy and Bobby who were obviously ready to start the journey. "Are you two strapping lads ready to go?"

They nodded somewhat impatiently.

"Then off we go." Roger turned to hug Pops, while Tommy and Bobby said their good-byes to Luke.

"You need anything before we leave?" Tommy asked Luke.

"Just keep that cookie safe and we'll share it together when all this is over," replied Luke.

He turned to Mary. Her eyes welled with tears, but she kept her head high.

"Don't cry," said Tommy.

"I cry a lot less than I used to," admitted Mary, "and I'm not sure if I like it that way or not."

"You're transforming, you know," said Tommy.

Mary smiled at him, a little confused. She wiped her eyes. "I transformed a few days ago. What do you mean?"

"Not that. That's just the way you look." Tommy stared at Mary like he was looking at her for the first time. "You're changing on the inside too. It's a good thing."

Tommy wrapped his strong arms around Mary. Then both of them spoke the same words in unison, "Be careful."

A second booming crash from within the forest interrupted the moment.

Roger jumped with a yelp. "What was that?" he asked.

"They are coming," Luke warned. "We have not a second to spare. The three of you must go." Tommy and Bobby looked to Pops.

"Go!" Pops screamed. "No more waiting. No time for good-byes!" Pops shooed the three travelers eastward.

Mary watched Tommy lead Bobby and Roger into the forest, toward the city. Luke grabbed her shoulders and turned her toward his face.

"Mary, I need you to go through the entire village and gather every mirror you can find," he ordered.

"Mirrors?" she asked.

"That's right. Tell the people that the Great King himself sent you and that you need all of their mirrors. Don't tell them why. There is not time to discuss the plan. Then tell them to leave their homes and get in the River. Tell them that their lives depend on it. Tell them that if they delay or enter the Lesser Forest today, that they will die."

"Die?" Mary was suddenly afraid again.

Pops grabbed her elbow. "Mary, do all that Luke says. We are at war now and you are a soldier. The enemy seeks to destroy all that we love and he is terribly real. We fight for the King and we will win, but we must act swiftly and without fear. Now go! Go!"

Mary summoned her courage and ran immediately to the tree

house a few hundred paces from Roger's home. She climbed the ladder and knocked on the door. An older lady in a nightgown called her inside.

Pops turned to Luke, "What now?" he asked.

Luke didn't hesitate. "We need to find out what that noise was, and more importantly, who caused it. You follow the crashing sounds and spy on their advance. Keep your distance, though. We don't need to be seen—not yet anyway. I have some preparations to make before Mary gets back. Let's meet back here in an hour."

Pops nodded and ran into the forest without saying a word. As soon as he hit the edge of the forest's canopy, most of the remaining light from the sky was cut off. The gray day became night in an instant. He could barely see the trees right in front of his face. So he did all he knew to do. He closed his eyes and followed the River within him. He sprinted into the pitch-black forest with his eyes tightly closed. All he could hear was her song.

Hand in Hand

A thick blanket of darkness covered the entire Lower Kingdom a few hours before dusk on the sixteenth day of the fourth month of the seventy-third year of Senkrad's reign. Within the Tree House Village no one could see more than a few feet without the aid of a lantern or candle. In the Lesser Forest, the darkness was so thick that it was impossible to see anything at all. It was as if the forest were growing at the bottom of a crevasse in a deep cavern, with no hope of ever receiving the light from above. In this dreadful black fog, Roger, Tommy, and Bobby found themselves blind and lost on their journey to warn the first of the endangered tree houses.

"I can't see a thing anymore," Tommy whispered to Roger and Bobby. "I don't know what to do." Roger opened his eyes at the sound of Tommy's voice, only to discover a more intense darkness waiting for him with his eyes opened than when they were closed.

"I cannot feel the River anymore," Roger admitted. "I don't know what to do either—I'm afraid that we are already lost." He spoke matter-of-factly.

"Why don't we just light a torch?" asked Bobby.

"I'm worried that the light from our torches will do nothing but attract the Phantoms and all other forms of evil, but perhaps there are no more options left for us," replied Tommy.

"I'll get mine from my bag," Bobby volunteered. Tommy heard his knapsack drop to the ground. Bobby rustled through his belongings. "Hold on—I need to take this glove off. I can't feel a thing."

He removed one of the wool gloves that he had been wearing since the journey began. Tommy felt Roger grab his arm.

"What is that, Bobby?" asked Roger, amazement in his voice.

"What is what? I can't see a thing."

"I don't see anything either," said Tommy. "What are you talking about, Roger?"

"You don't see that glowing orb of green light coming from Bobby's hand?" asked Roger. "It's coming from your left hand, Bobby. Right there! See?" Roger pointed at Bobby's gloveless hand, but neither Tommy nor Bobby could see him pointing. "I can see both of your faces in its light. Please, do not play games with an old man. Not now. You see it, right? Tommy?"

"I can't see anything, Roger," Tommy worried about his old friend. Was he seeing things that weren't there? "Are you not feeling well? Maybe we should stop and rest for a minute."

"Ouch!" Bobby grunted.

"What happened?" Tommy asked.

"I don't know. My finger is burning. Like it's on fire or something," he said.

Roger alone could clearly see everything. Bobby quickly removed the jeweled ring from his finger. Immediately the mysterious green light disappeared, leaving only the utter blackness and emptiness of the Long Night in Roger's eyes.

"What did you do with it?" asked Roger.

"What do you mean?" asked Bobby. "I didn't do anything. I just took off my ring. It was . . . burning me."

"What is that ring?" asked the old man.

"It's the ring that the Prince gave me before we entered the River to come down here. It was my gift . . . like Tommy's jacket." Bobby rolled the ring around in the palm of his hand—it still felt warm.

Tommy suddenly realized what had happened. "Put it back on, Bobby," he said.

Bobby slid the ring back onto his finger and Roger's eyes filled again with the green light. It was even brighter than before. "Amazing," he said. "It's the gift of light. Our Prince gave you the gift of light!"

"Why can't we see it, Roger?" asked Tommy.

"I don't know. Maybe you will in time. The important thing is that at least one of us has light, and at least one of us can access it. No doubt the light will remain hidden from the enemy as well. Bobby, come stand by me. Hold onto my arm so I can read the map and see the path. Don't let go. Tommy, you grab on as well. It's time to warn the others."

Roger saw Bobby reach out in the darkness, feeling for his arm. He grabbed his hand to pull him forward, and all at once, as soon as Roger touched Bobby's hand, the entire Lesser Forest lit up like a sun-drenched beach on the brightest summer day.

"Whoa!" exclaimed Roger. "Tell me you can see that now, boys."

"See what? It's still completely dark, Roger," confessed Tommy.

"Yeah, same for me. I can't see a thing. What do you see?" asked Bobby.

"Everything. I see everything, boys. Let's go!" With a newfound youthful enthusiasm, Roger led the young men through the forest by the illumination of Bobby's ring. They walked for less than thirty minutes in silence until Roger stopped suddenly, looked down at the map and glanced back up toward the hills in the distance.

"This way," he said, turning to his left. "We aren't far off now."

Roger led the young men onto a gently used path, over a rickety wooden bridge covering a small but strong stream, and past a few large evergreen trees.

As they crested a small hill, Bobby said, "I see something. Over there! Do you see it?"

"There's a light over there, Roger." Tommy squinted, trying in vain to get a clearer view. "Can you make out what it is?"

"Yes. I see more than just the light. It's the lantern from the porch of a tree house. This is the home of Simon and Helen. At least, it used to be."

"Does someone else live here now?" asked Tommy.

"I wish it were that simple, Tommy." Roger frowned and rubbed his forehead. "I'm afraid our friends still live here, but the rumor is that Simon has become someone else altogether. Regardless, let's warn them of the coming danger. They are, beyond whatever else they have become, still our friends."

The First Attack

A great distance away in the same forest, Pops knelt underneath the sprawling boughs of an ancient yew. He rubbed his tightly shut eyes. He had not opened them since he left the Tree House Village and entered the Lesser Forest, almost an hour before. The River had brought him to this place and then, as he had experienced at times before, her song had suddenly stopped. He could not hear or sense her at all, at least not in the way he was accustomed to hearing her.

He mumbled in whispers. "What should I do? What should I do? C'mon. Tell me something. Say something. Anything."

Though he could not feel the River, he could clearly sense the darkness surrounding him on all sides. He knew full well that the Long Night had begun and he felt his spirit grow fearful and confused.

"Pops?" an unfamiliar female voice startled him, causing his eyes to immediately pop open. In the imposed night he saw no one, no thing, only blackness. He waited in silence.

"Pops?" the voice returned, this time seeming to come from just over his left shoulder.

"Who's there?" he whispered.

There was no response, only a slight rustling in the branches.

"Who's there?" he repeated.

The unknown voice now seemed to come from directly behind him, and was barely audible. "There are two of them less than a hundred paces to your left. If you so much as move your foot, they will overcome you. Be still and do only as I say."

"Who are you?" Pops breathed.

"Salma," said the voice. "Now be quiet, or they will hurt you terribly."

To his left, Pops heard a rumbling and grunting in the blackness.

"Stay," Salma uttered.

From not far away, the dancing lights of torches illuminated the brush and trees. Whoever was out there was coming straight toward Pops. Their footsteps were heavy and menacing, crashing through the dense undergrowth.

Perhaps they don't have time to use the path, or maybe they just don't care, Pops thought. He could feel his heart racing and his hands sweating. He searched his mind for a plan, an idea, a voice—anything. Remembering that he had packed a hunter's knife in his belt, he slowly moved his right hand toward his left hip and secured the weapon.

"*Don't move,*" the unseen stranger insisted.

Pops tried to obey, but his hand shook in fear. The knife slipped from his grip and dropped to the ground, striking a rock with a loud clink.

Without warning, two dark figures pounced on top of Pops. They forced his face onto the floor of the forest and struck the back of his head.

"Kraxen basiped, hus!" He heard one scream in its own language.

"Basiped! Hus!" echoed the other as he struck the old builder again in the back of the head with the handle of his flaming torch. Pops stretched his hand back in an attempt to grab his knife that had fallen to the ground, but he instantly took one of the attacker's boots to his chin. The strike jarred a few of his teeth loose. His attackers kicked him mercilessly. Pops tasted his own blood in his mouth. His ears throbbed with his pulse and the pressure in his chest felt like a banging drum.

There was no chance of escape.

Turning his head back toward the tree's trunk to avoid another direct strike to the face, Pops started to lose consciousness. The last image he saw was the toe of a golden shoe, sparkling in the light of his attacker's torch and just peeking out from behind the large tree. One more blow landed on the back of his neck—and that was it. Pops closed his eyes and faded away.

Luke tied a small hand mirror to a low-hanging branch on a tree just behind Roger's tree house. Mary stood behind him, holding mirrors of various sizes in her arms. A lantern sat at her feet.

"Shouldn't Pops have returned by now?" she asked Luke.

"Yes. I thought he would have been back by now," he said, "but we can't wait any longer. Every mirror in the village must be tied to the outlying trees immediately." Luke pulled a candle from his pocket and tied it next to the mirror so that the two hung parallel, nearly touching each other. "This had better work," he muttered to himself.

"I don't really understand what we are doing," said Mary.

"I have a hunch," said Luke.

"A hunch?" asked Mary. "We're risking everything on a hunch?"

Luke turned to give Mary his full attention. He could see the fear in her eyes. "Yes," he said, "but it's an educated hunch." He smiled at Mary, then took a handful of candles from his coat pocket and gave them to her. "Take your lantern and some mirrors and tie them with the candles around the perimeter of the village south of here. Leave the other mirrors here for me." Luke bent down, lighting a torch from Mary's lantern while she stood motionless. "Mary, it will work. Do it now. Hurry," Luke ordered.

Mary ran off to the south. Luke inspected the hanging mirror and candle on the branch one more time. "You'd better work," he said to them. He looked into the darkness of the forest, hoping to see Pops returning. Luke gathered his supplies and walked northward along the bank of the River to prepare the village for the oncoming attack.

Magus

Light from inside Simon and Helen's home poured out of the windows into the blackness. Music and voices carried into the night from the tree house as well. It was obvious that there was some sort of party going on inside.

Simon's house seemed more like a small cottage than a traditional tree house. It had no ladder and was built in two stories from the ground under a huge and ancient tree. The tree itself made up the back wall of the house. It was similar to Roger's tree house, but three or four times larger. It was the largest tree house that Tommy had seen in either Kingdom.

Tommy followed Roger and Bobby up three wooden stairs and stood on a small porch in front of the door.

Roger turned and looked sternly at the two younger men. "Both of you, whatever unfolds tonight, just remember to question everything, but argue nothing. We aren't here to persuade or be persuaded about anything other than the coming trial we all shall face together."

Tommy nodded, having half-listened to Roger's instructions. He wondered who would throw a party on such a dark day? What kind of tree house *was* this?

At the sound of Roger's knock, the door immediately flew open.

An attractive older lady in a black evening gown stood on the other side. She locked eyes with Roger, and after an uncertain moment, threw herself into him, and hugged him tight around the neck.

"It's good to see you, Helen," said Roger.

"Magus! Roger is here!" the lady yelled back over her shoulder into her home, which the boys could now see was packed with well-dressed people of all ages. They laughed and ate and danced. The atmosphere was wholly different than the fearful darkness outside.

A tall and dignified man with silver hair and a chiseled chin approached from behind the lady. He wore a black tuxedo and flashed a brilliantly white smile. "Roger?" he said. "Come on in. I had no idea you were coming our way. What a great surprise. What a wonderful, unexpected surprise!"

"Thank you for your hospitality, Simon, but I haven't come alone," replied Roger. "These are two children of the King. Their names are Tommy and Bobby." Tommy half-bowed uncomfortably toward the distinguished gentleman. He had no idea why, but he felt drawn to the man.

"Well in that case, all of you come in! It's a cold and dark night out there. Perhaps a storm is coming this way," Simon looked out at the darkness as if noticing it for the first time. "Come in and eat and relax. My home is your home," Simon took hold of Roger's arm, pulling him inside, and Tommy and Bobby followed.

Everything about the home was regal and festive. Tommy's eyes adjusted to the lights. Lanterns and candles glowed from every wall, table, and mantel, and from the carved chandelier hanging above their heads. His ears rang with the sound of music and laughter. A pretty girl in a red dress winked at him and waved from the back of the room. He smiled and waved back.

"This is some party," said Bobby under his breath.

"Yeah," said Tommy.

"May I take your coats?" asked Helen politely. Bobby immediately removed his jacket and handed it to her. Roger followed suit more cautiously, checking the pockets for anything he might want to keep with him.

Without thinking, Tommy unbuttoned his jacket to remove it. Roger shot him a look so stern that Tommy actually felt his eyes burning upon him. He stopped suddenly before undoing the bottom button.

"I'll keep mine on, if it's all the same," replied Tommy. He glanced quickly to Roger, then back toward the hostess. "I'm still a little chilly from our journey."

"Suit yourself," she said, hanging the jackets on a coat rack near the front door. "Now, please, eat something. The kitchen is full of goodies." Bobby looked to Roger, who nodded like a father giving permission to his son. Then he walked over to a wooden table covered in various meats, salads, and desserts. There he sat down with several of the guests, introduced himself, and began to eat and talk with the others.

"Go get some food, Tommy," Simon said with a smile.

"Maybe in a second—I'm good for now, thanks," he said. He didn't want to miss anything Simon said.

The host stirred his drink with a small straw. "Are they new to this way of life?" he asked Roger.

"Very new," Roger replied.

"Are they going to build soon?" Simon surveyed Tommy's physique, staring at his worn jacket.

"I think so. That was the plan originally, anyway." Roger turned to face the man directly. "We need to talk, Simon." He looked all about the busy room. "In private, if that is possible," he added. "I'm afraid the news is more than urgent."

Simon looked cautiously at Roger before speaking. "Let's go to my study. Follow me."

"May I come?" asked Tommy.

Simon looked to Roger, and Roger returned his gaze.

"It's up to you. It's your house," Roger said.

"But it's your discussion," Simon scowled, dropping his cordial demeanor for the first time.

Roger looked at Tommy. "I have nothing to hide from you. Come along if you wish."

Simon led them past the banquet table toward a small staircase leading to the second level of the tree house. As they passed Bobby, Simon patted him on the head and said, "Eat away, son. What's mine is yours."

Roger, who was trailing behind, whispered to Bobby after Simon passed, "Don't overdo it. Be ready to leave soon."

The three men made their way through the crowded home and up the staircase. The second floor was quiet and simple compared to the ground floor. Simon lit an oil lamp on his desk and offered Roger a seat in a plain wooden chair. Simon sat behind his desk facing his guest, with his hands clasped in front of him.

"I'm sorry, Tommy," Simon said, not looking up. "I only have two chairs here. I usually don't have . . . observers to my private conversations."

Tommy squirmed. "I'm fine. I'll just stand back here."

"Suit yourself," he said. His voice was gruff. "What's the problem, Roger? Why are you here?"

Roger cleared his throat and began, "I know we have had our differences in the past, Simon, but—"

"Stop. Don't call me that," he snapped.

"I'm sorry?" Roger's eyebrows shot up.

"I don't go by that name anymore. It's a weak name," he responded.

"Very well, Magus," Roger replied. "I am not here to debate with you. You follow the Prince and the River as you see fit."

Simon rolled his eyes with a condescending smirk as Roger spoke. "You are not here to argue with me? You are not here to eat and receive our hospitality? So . . . why are you here, Roger? Are you here to show your new little learner boy how brave and adventurous you are?"

"I'm here to warn you," Roger replied.

"Warn me? Of what?" asked Simon, with a curious smile.

"The Dark Prince of the Lower Kingdom has initiated a ghastly and terrible plan to destroy us all. His army is on the move and coming your way. Phantom Messengers have been dispatched to destroy your tree house and all who call it home. You and all your people need to go back to the village and wait in the River for the Prince to rescue us. That is your only hope."

Magus laughed. "Phantom Messengers? Wading in the River? Have you been reading fairy tales again, Roger?"

"This fairy tale is more real than you can imagine," said Roger, standing to his feet.

"Nonsense," Simon said, also standing. "Tell Fred that I said hello. We are done here." Tommy's hands were shaking. He wished he had stayed with Bobby.

"Did you not notice the darkness today, Simon?" asked Roger.

"It's Magus," he corrected him through gritted teeth.

"Magus . . . right. Sorry. Did you not notice that it was darker than night when it should have been light outside this afternoon? Did you see the white ash falling from the sky before that? Did you not sense the River's song slowing to a faint rhythm in your heart?"

Roger's voice tightened as he pleaded to be understood. "This evil is as real as it gets, my old friend. Please, listen to me!"

Simon erupted. "There is no magic River! There is no magic song in your heart! There was no ash falling from the sky today, and this thick darkness is normal before a storm. You, my old friend, are simple and naive. You are my brother, the son of my King, but you are a foolish and stupid little child."

"Have you forgotten?" asked Roger. His voice shook.

"Forgotten what?" asked Magus, still enraged.

"That we are all children. Eternally seven," he replied.

"No, we aren't. You incredible fool. We were *once* children, Roger. Now we are adults." Magus glanced down at his desk, opened a drawer, and retrieved a small, square object. He held it to Roger's face from across the desk. "What do you see, sir? A seven-year-old child or a deceived, sad old man?" he asked, with a self-confident grin.

From where Tommy was standing, he could see Roger's reflection in the mirror as he looked at himself. Roger appeared as he normally did in the Lower Kingdom: an older man, with his intense eyes magnified by his round glasses. Tommy also caught sight of himself behind him. He felt suddenly uncomfortable seeing his dirty jacket in such a formal place.

Roger's eyes shifted in the mirror to see Tommy standing quietly in the corner. He turned to him.

"Are you ready to go, Tommy?" he asked.

Tommy just stared at him, frozen.

"I'm more than ready to go." Roger faced Simon, who now held the mirror to his side.

"I will see you again, my friend. It may be in another Kingdom, but I will see you again. And I will accept your apology at that time.

Mercy to you." Roger turned on his heels and walked toward the stairs leading down to the party. "Let's go, Tommy."

"Hey, Tom . . ." Simon's bright smile returned. He walked around his desk, keeping the mirror in his hand.

"Yes, sir?" Tommy replied.

"Take care of my old friend, here—and you are welcome to return anytime. Come back someday . . . when you grow up."

At those words, Magus's eyes filled with orange fire and Tommy instantly felt small. His heart throbbed with fear and his entire body grew cold. He trembled uncontrollably. He felt embarrassed to be so young in the presence of someone so mature. He felt naked and ridiculous. His vision clouded and he believed he was suffocating in his heavy jacket. He heard Magus laughing an evil laugh. Tommy ripped off his coat in a panic and fell to the floor in front of Roger. He grabbed onto his friend's leg, weeping. Roger quietly picked up the old jacket and wrapped it around Tommy as best he could. Magus walked over to the two of them, brushing lint from the sleeve of his tuxedo.

"I have some fine clothes that would fit a child, Tommy. If you'd like to try on a tuxedo, I'd be happy to give you one." Tommy looked up, confused and frightened. He wanted to be like Magus so much. So confident and grown-up. Full of power and in control. Tommy was so . . . insignificant. He reached for Magus as Roger tried to stuff his other arm into a sleeve.

"Move the jacket, Roger!" screamed Magus. "He's reaching for me."

"Never!" Roger yelled. He shook Tommy roughly. "Tommy, what did you promise the Prince about this jacket?"

Tommy was lost in confusion. Was he dreaming? This couldn't be real. Roger and Magus seemed like ghosts to him. He had never been so confused.

"What did you promise him, Tommy?" Roger asked again.

"That I wouldn't take it off," Tommy answered. The room spun around and around.

"Oh, surely he doesn't expect you to wear a dirty, hot jacket inside the warm home of a friend. It's rather rude, actually," said Magus. "Let me take it from you."

Tommy looked up at Simon. He loved every part of him. His tall body, his wise and deep voice, his strong hands reaching toward him. His dapper tuxedo. He was all that Tommy wanted to be, but wasn't yet: confident, influential—a leader.

And then Tommy looked into his eyes.

They were fiery, but cold. They were distant. They were the eyes of a dead man.

Tommy panicked and crawled to the corner of the room, completely covering himself in his jacket. He wept as he slipped his arms into the sleeves of the coat. His hands trembled as he fastened every button, right up to his neck.

Magus grew furious. His face reddened and the whole room grew warm. He turned on Roger, and a blazing stream of fire flew from his mouth and nostrils, causing Roger to jump back in fear. Simon's fingernails morphed into the talons of an eagle, and his long tongue split down the middle like a snake's. In a fit of rage, he struck the mirror against the corner of a nearby table and threw the shattered square at Roger's face. It sliced his cheek open before it fell in pieces to the floor.

Roger felt his face and examined the blood on his hands. Tommy looked up toward the two of them at the sound of the crash. His sanity returned, but he could not believe what Magus was becoming.

"Good-bye, Simon," Roger said calmly.

Once again, the man who had been Simon tried to correct him, but his voice had changed to something ugly and otherworldly. "It'sss Maggusssss!" he cried.

Tommy stood and slowly walked to Roger by the stairs.

"Hus, hus, hus . . . basipeds . . ." Simon was now mumbling what sounded like nonsense. He fell to his knees, spat up blood, and beat his head with his own hands, scratching his own face with his claws. His shirt was ripped and blood flowed freely from his nostrils.

Roger bent down next to the writhing monster and picked up the largest shard of the mirror he could find. He calmly held it in front of Simon's face.

Simon's eye caught his own reflection and he let out a screech so loud that the entire house heard it. Then the thing that had been Simon melted into a steaming puddle of black oil and grime.

In a matter of seconds, all that was left was a small lump covered in a hot, tarry liquid. Roger wiped off a section of the disgusting mess from the heap to reveal the face of a lifeless seven-year-old boy. He then looked behind him to see Helen in tears and several other party guests staring in confusion, with their mouths agape. He turned to Helen.

"Get every person in this house into the River by tomorrow morning, or you will die a worse death than this." Roger pushed his way through the stunned crowd and down the stairs. Tommy followed.

"What's going on?" Bobby asked. He had been standing at the foot of the stairs.

Tommy remained silent. He grabbed Bobby's arm and dragged him along. Roger snagged their coats at the door and exited the house to the sounds of a grieving wife and confused and scared party guests. He walked onto the porch into the darkness of the Long Night.

Tommy and Bobby looked at him in the light of the lantern. He was covered in black grime and his own blood. "Now you see what we are dealing with, Tommy?" he asked, putting on his coat. "Let's go. We should spend our time warning those who will listen."

At that, Bobby removed his glove and grabbed Roger's bloody hand.

"It's different this time," Roger said.

"What do you mean?" asked Bobby.

"The light. Everything is illuminated like before, but there is a green path on the ground. It must be the River leading us. Let's go."

He followed the lighted pathway with no need for a map. And Tommy and Bobby held onto each arm as he walked.

Through Roger's Eyes

After a three-hour hike through the darkness, Roger's aging legs grew so weary that he was forced to stop and rest. He stopped in a natural clearing at the top of a large hill and scanned the horizon. He followed the glowing pathway with his eyes as it turned eastward and meandered over another hill far off in the distance.

"I don't know where she is taking us," he told Tommy and Bobby as they held onto his jacket in the darkness. "The line must lead us on the safest route to the next tree house. Perhaps we should stop here and grab a few hours of sleep. This hilltop allows me to see in all directions in case of an oncoming attack."

"It's maddening," confessed Tommy.

"What are you talking about?" asked Roger.

"The darkness," Bobby answered for both of them. "It makes you crazy to have your eyes open for hours at a time and see nothing. It starts to play tricks with your head."

"Well, maybe we should start a small fire," said Roger. "That would warm us up and help you both see for a bit."

"But what about the Phantoms?" asked Tommy.

"What of them?" replied Roger. "The River has guided us this far, and she will continue to protect us. Let's have a fire and a good rest. We will resume our journey tomorrow morning."

"Is it still called morning when there is no sun?" asked Bobby.

"For us . . . yes. It is still called morning," Roger replied.

With Roger holding onto Bobby so he could see to gather wood, the three companions built a small fire on the hill. Then Roger was able to release Bobby, and they pulled some blankets from their packs. They huddled together in silence. Bobby was asleep within a matter of minutes.

"Get some rest, Tommy," Roger said. "I'll keep watch. Don't worry about anything."

Tommy closed his eyes. He was exhausted, but unable to sleep. "Roger, I'm sorry," he said, without opening his eyes.

"Sorry about what?" asked Roger.

"For today. For Magus. For . . . almost, you know . . ." Tommy sat up. "I let you down. I let the Prince down. I let everyone down."

Roger reached out his hand and grabbed Tommy's arm. "You removed your jacket for a few seconds," he said. "That's all that you did. You panicked. All is forgiven and we are all stronger for it now."

"No," said Tommy. "It is more than that. I didn't just remove my jacket . . . I almost trusted him. I mean, I really *wanted* to trust him."

"Of course you did," said Roger. "He's trustable, just not trust-worthy. All those people in his house trusted him. We all trusted him at one point. Simon is someone special—*was* someone very special. He was a lot like you, you know?"

"What do you mean?" asked Tommy.

"Well, for starters, he was given the same gift as you. The Prince only gives the humility jackets to powerful leaders. Until a few weeks ago, I only knew of two people to share in the privilege of wearing one: Pops and Simon. They both have that special thing about them, that thing that makes people want to trust them, to believe in them.

And so you were given the same gift because you have that same thing in you."

"I don't know . . . I don't think I have that—that thing. That whatever it is that makes people want to follow you. "

"You do, Tommy," Roger said. "You just don't really know how to use it yet. That's OK. You were given a great gift tonight. Now you know the options ahead of you. Do you want to become like Pops, or like Magus?"

"I hope Pops is OK." Tommy poked at a log in the fire.

"I'm sure he is," said Roger. But he secretly worried.

"So what happened to Simon? What happened to his jacket?" Tommy wanted to get his mind off what might be happening to Pops, or anyone else.

"I can't say for sure what happened to him or what became of his jacket, but I know that whatever happened to him happened after he traded his gift for that ridiculous tuxedo. It changed him over time . . . just small changes at first until he became what you saw in the end."

"A monster?" asked Tommy.

"Yes, a monster," Roger replied. "That, and an insignificant little puddle of goo on the floor. Just a black spot of nothingness."

"So, he is dead, then?" asked Tommy.

"Dead? Yes, he is dead . . . and no, he isn't. We'll have more answers about what happened to Simon in the Upper Kingdom after our journey here is complete," said Roger. "Magus, I believe, is dead. But I have a suspicion that Simon may live again somehow. These are the mysteries that the King and Prince speak to one another about. These discussions are beyond us. Now, go to sleep, Tommy. You will need your rest for tomorrow."

Tommy closed his eyes. Roger sat up and looked out into the darkness.

"Roger?"

"Yes?"

"What was your gift from the Prince? You've never spoken of it."

Roger smiled and turned his face toward Tommy's. The orange flicker of the small fire reflected on the perfectly round lenses of his eyeglasses. His kind, green eyes looked through them at Tommy, who had opened his eyes again. He tapped one of the lenses with his fingernail. "My glasses," he said. "They help me see people as they really are."

"So that is how you knew Magus was untrustworthy?" asked Tommy.

"I'm not sure I needed my glasses to see that," said Roger. "They help me see who *is* trustworthy more than who is not."

Tommy closed his eyes and after a few seconds, Roger thought he was asleep. Then came the sleepy voice, "How do your glasses work?"

Roger looked at Tommy and he saw him as he had always seen him, since the first day he crawled out of the River. Tommy was fast asleep before Roger could answer. "I see certain people and feel only . . . love," he replied, brushing a moth away from Tommy's face. "I feel so much love for them that it hurts my heart—that's when I know that the Prince trusts them, and I can too."

Roger closed his eyes as well, but never truly slept. He rested in the song of the River through the night and was overcome with a peace unlike anything he had felt since his last journey home to the Upper Kingdom, decades earlier.

Unseen by anyone, a complete company of seven messengers encircled their small camp throughout the entire night. They stood at attention, swords drawn, facing away from the children of the King and toward any possible threat that might be lurking in the night.

Village of Refuge

Luke and Mary had spent the entire night hanging mirrors and candles on most every low limb in the trees surrounding the tree houses. About eighty people lived in the tree houses of the village. They were somewhat accustomed to Pops and Roger (and their guests) involving themselves in unexplainable and strange matters, so some of them largely ignored Luke and Mary's frantic warnings of doom and destruction. Others, however, were so frightened by the unending darkness that they began to gather outside Roger's home to ask Luke and Mary what was happening.

They came, carrying candles and lanterns to light the way. Luke stood on a tree stump to see them all. "Please, everyone, listen to me! My name is Luke. I know that I am a new face to many of you, but I have come here directly from the Good Prince to warn you of a terrible disaster that has already begun. The Dark Prince of the Lower Kingdom has created this blackness and his intent is for it to never cease. He wants to imprison us all in this Long Night until we forget all about the warmth and power of the light from above. You must trust me now. The safest place for you to be is in the River. I encourage all of you to wade or swim in her waters until the Long Night is over."

Luke looked at Mary, who stood just behind him near the door of Roger's tree house, counting those who had gathered. "My partner and I have a plan to protect your homes, but you and your families will be safer in the River's waters than anywhere else."

"Where is Pops?" an older lady from the back of the crowd yelled up to Luke.

"He left yesterday to spy on the enemy and has not returned," said Luke. "That's all I know."

"What is so dangerous about this darkness?" asked another voice from the crowd. "I mean, it's annoying and all, but why do I have to go stand in the River? We all have lamps and lanterns and plenty of oil. Let's just stay in our homes until it passes."

"The darkness isn't the worst part of the plan," said Luke. "Senkrad has ordered an army of Phantom Messengers to destroy every tree house in the Lower Kingdom. We believe they will be here sometime today. Perhaps any minute now."

He heard them mumble to one another. It was a popular pastime to argue about the existence of messengers, but none of them had ever heard of Phantom Messengers. Luke watched helplessly while a few people walked back toward their homes, shaking their heads in frustration.

"You have all been warned!" Luke called over their chatter. "Make your decisions, but I'm pleading with you to swim in the River today. What would it hurt to go for a swim even if none of this happens?"

"It will be freezing cold, for one thing!" yelled Leo, an older resident of the village who kept to himself and had very few friends. Mary recognized his voice. He had been the only resident of the village who had refused to give her a mirror, claiming he had none.

"No, it's not true. I have been in the water. It's warm now," said Luke, with a hint of frustration.

More people laughed at him and the crowd began to move away

in all directions. Three younger residents immediately came forward and asked Luke how they could help protect the village, but very few people actually jumped into the River—a total of eight. Luke had Mary give torches to those who volunteered to help, while he explained the battle plan to them.

"We have prepared the wood and fuel for a large bonfire near the pier," he said. "Mary or I will light the fire when it is time for us to take action. I need all of you to take an area of the village and light all of the candles hanging from tree limbs in your area as soon as you see the fire ignited. These candles will illuminate mirrors that will protect the tree houses."

"How will mirrors protect us?" asked one of them.

"Just trust me," said Luke. "This is what I do."

From there, Mary assigned each torch carrier to a watching area near their station where they could also see the pier. Then they ran off to their places.

"You ready for this, Mary?" Luke asked.

"Nope," she smiled. "I haven't been ready for anything that has happened since I jumped into the River weeks ago."

Luke smiled back. "I'm tired," he confessed. Suddenly they were interrupted by a loud rustling in the trees behind Roger's house.

"They're here!" Mary whispered in a panic. Luke put a finger to his mouth to silence her and carefully looked around the edge of the tree house. He heard many voices whispering to one another.

"Is this it?" a voice asked from within the forest.

"I think so," another female voice responded.

"Go light the fire, Mary!" Luke gave the signal.

Mary started off at a run toward the pier.

As soon as Mary left, a young man with slick dark hair and dressed in a dirty and tattered tuxedo emerged from the woods. He was followed by an older lady wearing a torn evening gown and carrying a nearly expired torch.

"Who are you?" asked Luke.

"I am Helen, a friend of Roger's," she replied. "My tree house was destroyed and my husband is dead." Many more formally dressed people began to pour out of the forest. They appeared exhausted, some with obviously serious wounds to their heads and bodies. A few just stared into the distance with blank looks on their faces.

Luke turned toward the River and bellowed, "Don't light the fire, Mary! They are with us! DON'T LIGHT THE FIRE!"

THE LAST BATTLE

One Fight at a Time

Mary was only a second from lighting the bonfire when she heard Luke and turned to see the last of the party guests exiting the forest, carrying a wounded lady on a makeshift stretcher. She closed her eyes in sorrow. What in the world had happened to these poor people?

In hopes that Tommy might have returned with the refugees, she ran back to Luke only to find more than a dozen scared and wounded people whom she had never seen before. She felt so sorry for them, she didn't mind speaking up.

"All of you who are able, follow me to the River," she said. Those who could walk followed her, while some stayed with Luke.

She brought them to the edge of the pier.

"Just jump in," she said. "Her water is warm tonight."

As soon as they hit the water, their small cuts and scrapes began to heal. Those with bigger injuries were also healed, but at a slower rate.

Helen was the last to come to the pier's edge. "I haven't been in the water in years," she admitted. "I don't know if this is a good idea."

Mary saw her fear and the grief in her eyes. "It's been a hard night for you," she said.

Helen broke down and grabbed Mary. "My husband is dead!" she cried.

Mary hugged her and stroked her hair. "This is a bad day, but you are safe now. Come on and get in."

"So many died . . . during the attack," Helen continued, speaking through her sobs. "And some were captured by those . . . creatures. But your friends! They saved us!"

"My friends?" asked Mary.

"Roger and the two younger men," she was beginning to catch her breath. "They warned us to come to you. Thank you for saving us."

"You're welcome," said Mary. "But it is really the Prince who saved you. He is the one who sent us here to help you."

Helen stepped back. "Really?"

"Yes, he sent us here a few months ago."

"He still remembers me?"

Mary smiled. "He never forgets." She took Helen by the hand and led her down into the River.

News of the arrival of the refugees spread quickly throughout the entire Tree House Village. Most who were suspicious of Luke's warning came back to the River to see the wounded and hear first-hand accounts of the Phantoms' attack on Simon's tree house. As a result, most residents were persuaded to enter the River's waters. They were shocked to find the waters warm and calming, though the dark night was cold and menacing. Many were eased to sleep as they floated on their backs near the pier in the River.

The most distant tree house southward belonged to Leo, the recluse who was one of the first to leave the gathered crowd hours earlier. He watched the people entering the River from the window of his tree house until, in his frustration, he pulled his heavy drapery closed and mumbled, "Fools—all of them. Like lemmings flying off a cliff. Who jumps into a cold river in the middle of the night?"

He blew out the candle by his bed and retired for the night, though it was actually still morning. Like many others, he was losing track of day and night.

At the pier, Luke continued to help the last of the residents of the village into the River's waters. Mary jogged down the pier as he was lowering an elderly lady into the water from the edge of the boardwalk. The lady was knee-deep in the water but refused to let go of Luke's hands as he stood above her on the pier.

"Don't be nervous, ma'am. The River will comfort you once you are in the water," said Luke, in a calming voice.

"But I can't swim!" she screamed.

"Have you never been in the water before?" asked Luke.

She shook her head no.

"Then how did you originally get into the Tree House Village?"

She continued to cling onto his arm. "What do you mean? I've lived here my whole life—as long as I can remember," she said, nearly losing her grip.

"I couldn't swim the first time I entered the River either," confessed Mary, who was now standing beside Luke. She had her hands on her knees, bending down to get closer to the lady's face. "Just let go," Mary whispered. "She wants to take care of you."

The lady's face softened as she looked at Mary. She closed her weary eyes and let go of Luke's hands. She fell into the pool that gathers from the River with a huge splash, and then quickly sprang up to catch her breath.

"It's warm!" she shouted with a smile. She slowly swam over to the center of the waters to meet her friends.

"Did you see that?" asked Mary.

"Yeah, she could swim after all," said Luke.

"No, not that," said Mary. "She grew younger when she went in . . . by at least twenty years."

Luke grinned, watching the lady hug and laugh with her friends as they floated in the waters of the River.

"I'm starting to feel kind of old the longer I stay down here," Mary said.

Luke touched her arm, "You don't look any older to me. Besides, we'll be home soon."

Another deafening cracking sound came from just within the forest behind Roger's tree house. Luke spun on his heels and ran up the pier toward the noise.

"Luke?" Mary ran after him, watching him hurry to the unlit bonfire on the River's bank.

Then the tree containing Roger's tree house fell with a huge crash into the common area of the village. Gasps and shouts came from the people in the River, though her waters remained calm.

"Everyone stay in the River! You too, Mary! Get in!" Luke screamed over his shoulder. He lit the bonfire with the touch of a torch as he passed it and ran on toward Roger's house.

"Oh, my King," Mary whimpered. Her ears filled with the thunderous cracks and splintering sounds of her friend's home breaking into pieces. She stood stunned and motionless on the boardwalk. Within three seconds, the bonfire blazed into a fiery mound. Instants later, dozens of tiny flames from the candles they had hung became visible all along the outskirts of the village. Then, as suddenly as the first tree, a second tree fell. This time it was in the direction of Leo's tree house. Mary heard a scream of pain.

She raced that way without a second thought.

Luke had arrived at Roger's fallen home. In the growing illumination of the massive bonfire, he saw them for the first time—dark creatures, with skin that resembled the scales of a black snake. They wore tanned leather armor and carried clubs, swords, and lit torches.

Snorting like pigs, they spoke in an ugly language. Luke understood this to be the ancient language of the Dark Prince, something he had read about in his studies, though he had only heard bits of it when he was imprisoned in the Palace of the Lower Kingdom. One of them, the largest, turned his attention away from dismantling Roger's house and stood to face Luke as he approached. He had glowing yellowish eyes with elongated pupils that stared through Luke with an other-worldly evil coldness.

"Hut, hus, hut . . ." he seemed to be mumbling to himself. Then he turned to the others and barked out some sort of a command: "Basiped, hus!" His companions, who were on their knees ripping the wall of Roger's home into shards of fuel for Senkrad's furnace, silently rose to their feet. With the exception of the first one, who was a foot taller than the others, they were all about seven feet tall with bulging muscles and protruding potbellies.

Luke braced himself for their attack. He slipped his left hand into his jacket pocket and held his torch in front of his face as if it were a sword. "This is your only warning!" he yelled in their direction. "Leave now or we will destroy you all!"

The first Phantom, the largest, drew a heavy, two-handed sword from a leather scabbard on his belt and confidently walked toward Luke while the other Phantoms stayed behind, seeming to lose inter-est in such an insignificant enemy. He walked straight to Luke and stopped within three feet of his flaming torch. Without so much as a grunt, he lifted his sword above his head with both hands to strike down the child of the King. Luke calmly pulled a small hand mirror from his pocket and held it out within inches of the monster's face.

"This is what you truly are," Luke stated. He felt no fear.

The Phantom stared, perplexed, at the mirror. He dropped his sword, tilting his head to one side like a curious puppy. With a terrible look of self-disgust he touched his hand to his mouth. Then, starting with his nose and lips, he began to dissolve and melt, as if he were made of candle wax. He eventually morphed into a formless puddle of mysterious black goo at Luke's feet. All that remained, apart from the liquid mess, was his armor and massive sword. Luke carefully walked around the steaming tar and approached the other three Phantoms who had gone back to destroying Roger's home, not noticing their leader's destruction.

"Hey, you frauds!" Luke cleared his throat. They all looked up at him from where they crouched. He held his mirror in front of their faces, one by one. Each Phantom melted at his feet like an ice cube on a sidewalk on a hot summer day. Only their armor, shields, and weapons remained amidst the boiling goo.

Just then two of the girls who had previously volunteered to light the candles came running to Luke.

"It's working!" one of them said. "The Phantom Messengers . . . they are, well, they are *melting* all around the perimeter of the village. I've never seen anything like it!"

"Only two of the tree houses fell," said the other. "Your plan is working!"

It was in that moment that Luke turned his attention to Leo's fallen tree house. He tried to peer into the darkness, but he could see nothing but shadows.

"Come with me," he said to one of the girls. To the other he ordered, "Gather their armor and helmets—we may have use for them."

He carefully approached the remains of the tree house with his mirror held ready at his side. The house was a complete shambles— only some shattered dishes and torn bedding indicated a person had lived in this spot at all. Most of the substantial beams of the house had been stripped away and carried off. What was left looked more like kindling than walls. Luke kicked around some pieces of broken furniture and lifted up some branches. No sign of life. He also noticed that, unlike all the other tree houses in the village, this one was in complete darkness with no candles anywhere near.

"Why didn't we light candles around this one?" Luke asked the girl following him.

"We tried," she said. "But when we got to them, they were gone. The old guy who lives here must have taken them down."

"I suppose we can only help those who want to be helped." Luke looked into the forest as he spoke. "I think they may have carried him off along with the wood."

"And the girl too?" she asked.

"What girl?"

"Your friend—Mary. I saw her running this way when the house went down."

Luke snapped his eyes back toward the girl. "Are you sure?"

She nodded. Luke's shoulders drooped for a moment, but he straightened himself and strode away toward the River. He needed to talk to the crowd in the River and explain what had happened. This wasn't a time for panic.

The girl followed close behind. "Aren't you going to go looking for her?"

Luke turned without breaking his pace. "One fight at a time. What's your name?"

"I'm Claire."

Luke kept moving. "Well, Claire, we can only fight one battle at a time. We have a frantic crowd to control and an entire defense system to reconstruct. Once that's done, I'll go look for Mary. But knowing her, and the way of the Good Prince, I'm sure she will stay safe."

To himself he added, "I hope."

A Little Hope

When the massive tree had fallen, Leo's tree house had splintered into thousands of pieces.

"Hello? Sir? Are you all right?" Mary approached the tree cautiously. Though the bonfire was beginning to light up much of the village, this particular tree was on the southernmost tip of the community, far enough away to remain mostly in shadows. Mary was without a torch and could only make out shadowy images as she searched for a survivor. She climbed into the mangled tree house, sliding carefully through a shattered window that had only a few bits of rough glass left at the edges. From somewhere under the rubble, a moan came.

"Sir, is that you?" she asked.

"Help . . . me . . ." Leo gasped for air under the weight of the tree.

"Where are you? I can't see very well," She felt through the tree limbs in the darkness.

"Over here . . ." the man's voice grew even more faint as he managed to reach a hand up toward Mary's leg. She bent over and tried to remove the debris surrounding him. "Hang in there, Leo," she said, grabbing his hand.

"Be . . . careful . . ." Leo was weak and fading. Mary could barely hear him.

"Hold on, we are going to get you out of this—"

Instantly the shadowy darkness turned utterly black for Mary. She felt some kind of rough, scratchy cloth on her face and something pulled tight around her neck. Two huge and powerful hands grabbed her around the waist and jolted her up high into the air. She let out a muffled scream, but nobody could hear her cry for help. Without warning, her captor then threw her headfirst onto the cold ground. With a hollow thud she lost consciousness.

When she came to, she had no idea where she was or how long she had been unconscious. The cloth sack was still covering her head, but it had now glued itself onto her face with the dried blood coming from her wounded forehead. She tried to move her hands up to her face, but they were tied securely behind her back. Her feet were also bound together. Realizing that she was completely helpless, she loudly burst into tears.

"Who's there?" A raspy voice came, not far from Mary's feet. She quickly became silent. Then, gathering her courage, she asked, "Who are you? Where are we? Please . . . let me go."

"I'm afraid I can't let you go," said the voice. "I'm chained and blindfolded. I've been stuck here for several hours, maybe days."

The voice was weak, but so familiar. "Pops?"

"Yes? Who's there?" he said. "Mary! Is it you?"

"Yes! It's me. I can't believe it's you . . . I was so afraid you were lost, or . . ."

"Not dead," said Pops. "Though being stuck here is almost worse—knowing a war is going on out there without me."

"Where are we?" she asked.

"I have no idea. They jumped me and brought me here. Every so often one of them comes in through a heavy door behind me. You can hear his footsteps coming down a corridor about ten seconds before he opens the door with his keys. Sometimes he brings food. Sometimes he asks me questions in his language, but I can't understand what he is saying."

"Is he a Phantom?" asked Mary.

"That has been my assumption. I haven't actually seen him, though. When he brings food, he releases one of my arms so that I can eat, but when I tried to remove the blindfold, he struck me on the face. Enough of my problems, though—tell me some good news, Mary. How is it going out there?"

"I wish I had more good news to tell." She tried to roll herself into a better position. "I was captured as they started their attack on the Tree House Village. They destroyed Roger's and Leo's tree houses, but beyond that I don't know anything else. Luke was fighting them off with mirrors. He says they can't stand their own reflections."

Pops was silent for a while, then he said, "And Tommy? Have you heard from him?"

"No . . . but a group of people came to the River from one of the distant tree houses. Roger and Tommy had sent them to us for protection, so I know they are out there, somewhere. The people came out of the forest all dressed up in gowns and tuxedos, like they were coming from a wedding or something."

"That would be Simon's clan," said Pops. "That's interesting. Simon went into the River, huh? I never thought I would see the day when he would humble himself enough to return—"

"No, Pops," Mary interrupted. "Luke said that their leader, Simon, was killed. His wife and some of his friends survived the attack, but he did not." She adjusted her body, using what felt like a wall to help her get to a sitting position. She heard Pops sigh. "I'm sorry, Pops," she said. "Was that man a friend of yours?"

"He wasn't much of a friend anymore . . . but still my brother. This is terrible—and me, stuck in this hole." Mary could hear the frustration in his voice. "Maybe this is truly the end for us all."

"Some are being saved." Mary tried hard to sound cheerful, even though her head was throbbing. "Some are being saved right now—that is the good news, Pops. Many tree houses will be saved because of Luke's planning. As far as we know, Tommy, Bobby, and Roger are safe and rescuing many people. Somewhere between seventy and eighty children of the King were wading in the River when I was last there. People who never trusted her before today are swimming and laughing in her waters. And you are alive, Pops! *We* are alive and reunited and going to get out of these chains and back home to the Upper Kingdom where we belong. There is good news, Pops. It's all around us."

Pops nodded his head in agreement, though Mary couldn't see him. "You are a gift from the Great King himself . . . and you are maturing beyond my wildest dreams. You are right . . . there is good news, indeed. Forgive me."

There was silence in the cell for a few minutes. Then Pop asked, "Mary, your gift from the Prince—you still have it, don't you? They didn't take it from you?"

Mary could feel the chain around her neck. "Yes, it is still with me. I guess they weren't interested in jewelry."

"I remember the day you saw your transformed self in that little locket mirror."

"Yes, I often look in it, not to see myself, but to see the word inscribed inside. It reminds me of the Upper Kingdom, and I can picture myself back there someday."

"Hmmm. The reflection of hope. Sounds like what we need about now," said Pops. And in the dark, his face broke into a broad smile. "Yes, indeed, a little hope could go a long way here!"

Mary heard the smile in his voice and wondered for a minute at his change in mood. She leaned forward and felt her locket dangling against her chest. *The reflection of hope.* As understanding slowly came to her, she smiled too in the darkness.

Alex and Campbell

"**A**re you awake finally?" Roger handed Tommy a few crackers and some cheese. "Hurry up and eat . . . we have places to go today."

Tommy didn't normally have cheese for breakfast.

"Go on and eat it. It's all I brought with me," Roger said.

Roger shook Bobby awake, giving him the same breakfast. The boys ate as Roger began to pack their bags for them.

"Is it morning?" asked Bobby.

"Yes, late morning. You both slept for a very long time . . . maybe ten hours. I'm afraid the Long Night may also cause people to continually oversleep. Too many days of it, and everyone in the Lower Kingdom will be sleeping their lives away."

Roger extinguished the fire, causing the world to grow eerily dark again to Tommy.

"Can you see the path again?" he asked Roger.

"Give me your hand, Bobby . . . good . . . yes, it's still there. Let's go."

The green pathway, which Roger called "the Line," led them in all directions throughout the entire expanse of the Lesser Forest. After walking for about two hours, Tommy finally saw a speck of light in the distance.

"I see something," he said.

"Yes," said Roger. "There is a small tree house just ahead with a candle lit in the window."

Tommy and Bobby waited below as Roger climbed the ladder in darkness and knocked on the hatch in the floor. The light of an oil lamp flooded the darkness as the door opened up. Without entering the tree house, Roger warned the man and woman living there of the coming destruction. He sternly ordered them to return to the River. Tommy heard him say, "I am not asking, I am commanding you in the name of the Great King to enter the River." Then he climbed down the ladder and grabbed Bobby's hand. They closed the hatch and again Tommy's vision went black.

"Do you think they will go?" asked Tommy.

"Yes. I think so, but it is not our job to make them obey," said Roger. "We are sent to tell the story we have been given—as terrible as it is. That's all we can do. Let's go. Time is our enemy now."

The three walked for twelve hours that day, covering many miles as they zig-zagged all throughout the valley. From time to time, the Line brought them to the very edge of the city, but never crossed into it. They had warned a total of eleven houses that day, five of which Roger had no idea even existed. Somehow they had just sprung up. The newer, previously unknown tree houses were the most receptive to Roger's message, though all of them at least listened because of the reality of the unending darkness that was impossible to deny.

The twelfth tree house they came to was brand new and quite large. It belonged to a tall man named Alex and his wife, Campbell, who had the look of someone who spent a lot of time in the kitchen. Her broad smile spread between rosy cheeks as she urged all three of the travelers to come in and eat supper with them before continuing on their journey. At first, Roger refused to accept their invitation because, as he explained, the task before them was now even more urgent. But the hosts were so persuasive, and his feet so tired, that he eventually agreed to come in for a few minutes.

The tree house was warm and comfortable, with candles all around giving welcome light to Tommy's eyes. Alex brought his guests into the combined kitchen and dining area and had them sit at a newly constructed table. Campbell's shining silver apron reflected the glow from the kitchen oven, and her plump figure flew about the room with balletic grace and purpose as she prepared food, and generally made everyone feel at home.

"Alex, it is a pleasure to meet you, and I think I can speak for all of us and say we appreciate your hospitality, but you and your wife must leave now and go to the River," warned Tommy. "Please—if you are worried about us, let us take your food with us and eat as we go."

Alex replied, "Tommy, we will stay here and eat with you. Then you will each sleep here for the night. We have already prepared three cots for you in the upper level. Once you have all fallen asleep with full bellies, in warm beds, then Campbell and I will walk to the River."

"What do you mean, you *prepared* cots for us?" asked Bobby.

"We were told to wait here until the King sent three messengers. We were clearly instructed to feed them and give them beds, and then—and only then—do whatever they asked of us. Of course, we expected actual Messengers of the Great King, but now we see that you are children of the King, like us, sent with a very real and dreadful message."

"Who told you all these things?" asked Roger.

Alex smiled. "The Prince himself, nearly a week ago."

The room grew silent with reverence. Campbell brought in a

plate of freshly baked rolls with butter and jam. She sat them on the table.

"You apron is like nothing I've ever seen before," said Tommy. "It seems to glow and change form when you move."

"Yes," said Campbell with a smile. "It was my gift from the Prince. I love it." She turned back toward the kitchen to finish preparing the stew for the main course.

"What does it do?"

Campbell looked back at Tommy and smiled with a wink. He couldn't help but smile back at her. Something about her eyes made Tommy feel safe again, like he was sitting with the Prince on the patio of the Palace of the Great King. "It does that," she said. "Whatever it just did to you . . . there are no words for it."

"Are any of you married?" asked Alex.

Tommy laughed. "No," he said. Bobby giggled like a little boy again.

"They're relatively new down here, Alex," said Roger.

"Ah. I suppose it is a funny concept your first year down here," he said. "Sometimes a man and a woman just become best friends and want to live their lives together."

Bobby stared at Tommy.

"What are you looking at?" he asked. He could feel his cheeks growing warm.

"Who is your best friend, Tommy?" he asked.

"I have a lot of friends," he said. "You for one. Roger. Pops."

"And?"

"And Mary."

Alex and Campbell looked at each other. Roger laughed deeply.

"We're just friends," Tommy declared.

"Good," said Alex. "That's the way to do it." He winked at

Tommy. Tommy wanted to crawl under the table. He also wanted to see Mary very badly.

"She is special," he said. He looked out the window into the darkness and cold mist. "I just hope she's OK. She's supposed to be at the River, where it meets the Tree House Village."

"We'll see her tonight then, Tommy," said Campbell. "We'll let her know that you are thinking of her."

Tommy said nothing. He nodded shyly and smiled to say thanks. Then he kicked Bobby under the table.

They ate until their bellies were full and their hearts were warm, then Alex and Campbell led them upstairs to three beds overflowing with blankets and pillows. They said their good-byes and exchanged hugs.

"When you get to the River, tell Mary that we are safe," said Tommy, hugging Campbell.

"I will, Tommy," she said. "I can't wait to meet her."

Alex and Campbell silently packed a few belongings and left their newly constructed home without a torch or lamp to give them light. They held hands, closed their eyes, and followed the River's song for hours until they felt the warmth of the huge bonfire on their faces.

Opening their eyes, they were met by the smile of a confident young lady. "I'm Claire," she said. "Welcome back to the River."

Alex and Campbell looked past Claire to see the pool that collects from the River filled with people.

"How many are here?" Alex asked.

"We quit counting at two hundred," said Claire.

"Where is Mary?" asked Campbell with a smile.

Claire looked past the newcomers to see Luke standing behind them. He came forward and put his arms around Alex and his wife. "Mary is on a mission," he said. "Come, get in the River's waters. You need to warm up."

"You must be Luke?" asked Alex.

"That's right," Luke replied.

"I have a message from one of your friends—he said to tell you that he is proud of you and that he can't wait to see you when this is over."

Luke smiled. "That's nice. Thank you. Was it Roger or Tommy?"

"Neither," said Alex. "It was the Good Prince."

Luke's eyes grew wide with surprise at first, and then softened. He quickly looked away toward the River and up the mountainside.

Alex gave Luke a slap on the back and led his wife into the River. They knew the way.

Welcome to Zakum

The faint glow of Bobby's ring woke Roger from an exhausted sleep. The upper room of Alex and Campbell's tree house was bathed in the ring's green light. Tommy and Bobby slept soundly in their cots on both sides of him. He had no idea how long he had been sleeping, or if it was morning or evening, but he knew it was time to get moving.

"Time to get up, boys," Roger said in a loud voice. They both opened their eyes.

"Waking up is terrible," said Tommy in a deep, morning voice. "At least there is light in my dreams."

Roger lit a candle, giving light to the small room for the other two. "We can't waste any time. I'll fix a quick breakfast while you wash up and pack. We leave in fifteen minutes."

"Is it morning for sure? How long did we sleep?" asked Bobby.

"I don't know anymore, Bobby," said Roger. "I'm losing track now. Don't worry, though. The King knows. Now, hurry and get ready for whatever today will bring us."

A few minutes later, the three of them were in their familiar traveling formation, with Tommy and Bobby holding onto Roger's arms as he followed the Line, never questioning where it was leading.

Suddenly Roger stopped. "I had no idea we were this close."

"To the palace?" asked Tommy.

"The city. I can see it from here. The palace is close also, but the Line is taking us past it, into the lowest point of the city."

"I wish I could see the city," said Bobby.

"No you don't, Bobby. It's . . . empty. What little beauty it had is gone."

"I never thought it had any beauty." A look of disgust passed over Tommy's face.

"The people, Tommy. The people are missing. All I see are the buildings now. Let's go. You've got to be prepared for anything, boys. We might as well light our torches now. We can't expect to just walk in unnoticed in any case."

The torches illuminated the trees around them, but Tommy still could not see the city in the near distance. The black fog around them was just too thick.

"Let's go," said Roger. "I still need your hand to see the Line, Bobby."

Tommy noticed the trash and debris on the ground as they drew closer to the city. It seemed even worse than before. The Line brought them down the main thoroughfare in the center of town. It was the same street with the diner, where Bobby first accepted the invitation from Tommy to live in the Upper Kingdom. Tommy looked toward Bobby as they walked past the darkened and empty diner, but Bobby did not react at all.

"Bobby, this is where we met. Do you remember?"

"Tommy," Roger cautioned, "this isn't the time for that."

But Tommy was determined. "He should know."

"What are you talking about?" asked Bobby.

Tommy stopped in the middle of the street and closed his eyes. He could hear it—the River, singing the way she had the first day he met her. He did not really understand why, but he knew it was time for Bobby to remember. He took Bobby's hand and covered it with his own, just as the Prince had done to him that day in the diner. Bobby looked confused at first, then as his mind flooded with memories, expressions of pain, joy, anger, sadness, and finally, peace passed over his face.

He saw his brothers, his father's funeral, his old friends. He saw the day he was fired from his job . . . and he saw Tommy in the diner, offering him a new home. A single tear cut a silvery path down his dark cheek. He put his hand on Tommy's shoulder and shook him gently. "Thank you, thank you. Thank you, my friend."

"It was the King and the Prince who helped you . . . not me. I just introduced you."

"But you made me see—I can see now. I can see it all. Why—why things were the way they were. Why they are the way they are, with me at least. I can see better than I've ever done before. You showed me how."

Roger stood still, just staring at the two young men. He could hear the River's song grow louder. Suddenly, at the moment Bobby stopped talking, the entire city lit up, like a giant spotlight had just been switched on. Roger watched as the two friends looked in all directions. He saw Tommy pointing down the path into the lower regions of the city.

The Line visible only to Roger for days now shone in the eyes of both Tommy and Bobby.

"The Great King has shown us all how to see," Tommy said. "We don't need our torches anymore."

Bobby extinguished his torch on the ground. "Roger, what about you? Are you from this place too?"

"We are all from here, but it is not our home. Not anymore."

"And this place is not where our journey ends. Let's get going." Tommy hiked his pack up on his shoulders and led the way, following the Line. Bobby followed, and Roger brought up the rear this time.

"May the Great King keep his vision unclouded," Roger said to himself.

After a short time, the Line brought them right up to the rickety gates of a repulsive junkyard. Tommy bent back the damaged wire fencing and motioned to Bobby and Roger to go inside. They both covered their mouths and noses as they stepped through. The air reeked with a sulfuric, sickening smell of burnt flesh and spoiled eggs. Wild dogs slunk between heaps of scrap, which rose like massive metallic stalagmites from the ground. Rolls of rotting trash had to be walked over to find the way of the Line. In the very center of the garbage dump, the Line simply stopped as it dissolved into the base of a mound of refuse.

"Where are we?" asked Tommy.

"This must be Zakum," said Roger. "It's the lowest part of the valley. All the trash from the city ends up here as well as . . . other things."

"What kinds of 'other things'?" asked Bobby. For once, he looked as though he was not ready for the adventure to come.

"Dead things," said Roger.

"Well, if they're dead, they can't bother us then." Tommy kicked around some oil-soaked cardboard boxes at the bottom of the heap. "What we need to worry about now is why the Line is stopping in the middle of this disgusting place for no apparent reason." He walked a few paces around the massive mound. "What do you think? Can we move it?"

Bobby slowly approached the pile of trash. It was about ten feet high and twenty feet wide. The garbage collected there seemed a bit more organized than the other piles. It was more or less in the shape of a giant cube. The Line ran straight into a discarded old metal door—like something from a public restroom. It was yellowish and corroded on the bottom, with broken hinges on one end. It looked as if it might fall off at the slightest touch.

Bobby reached out a finger and slowly stretched it toward the door. As soon as Bobby touched the door, it shot out toward him, bloodying his nose and sending him flying several feet backward. From the hole where the door had been, three figures jumped out so quickly that Tommy could make no sense of them. One of them jumped Tommy. Tommy swung his fists at the empty air, but it only took a split second for his assailant's knee to crash into his stomach. He bent in pain, only to receive an elbow to the back of his head. He fell face first to the ground and his attacker sat heavily on his back, leaving him motionless and defeated. Though he didn't see what happened, by the sounds around him and the glimpses he caught of arms and legs, he knew Roger and Bobby had been overcome in a similar fashion.

Tommy could barely breathe as his attacker pressed a knee into the base of his neck, mashing his face into the rancid trash on the ground. "Who are you?" demanded a stern female voice.

"Armm . . . tarrrmy," he tried to speak, but it was nearly impossible. The woman pulled his hair back, lifting his head so that he could be heard. "My name is—Tommy and I—am a child—of the Great King." Tommy gasped for breath.

The pressure on the back of Tommy's neck eased, and his attacker let go of his hair. Standing to her feet, she said, "Umm . . . sorry, Tommy."

Tommy rolled on his back. He looked up at a tall and strong young woman with short, curly hair and wild eyes. Tommy stared at her in confusion, his head still spinning from his beating. She held out a hand to help him up, and the two other girls released their captives.

"It's me . . ." she said with a wince, grabbing Tommy's hand.

Tommy wiped the blood and rotting garbage from his mouth. Who was this crazy girl?

"Amanda. It's Amanda. Remember me? I'm really sorry. It's just that we were expecting them . . . so, you know? Hurry up. Come inside. All of you. We can talk there."

Taking the Pseudo

Tommy held a puddle of his own blood in his hand. He watched as Amanda and her friends scrambled about their home, searching for medical supplies. All three of them were dressed the same—black, long-sleeved tunics, mottled gray-green pants, and heavy, black boots.

"Sorry," said the one who had attacked Roger. She had shiny black hair and dark, almond-shaped eyes. "I'm Kelly, this is Samantha."

Samantha, a younger girl with spiky red hair, waved and looked at Bobby, "Sorry about your nose," she said with a grimace.

The inside of Amanda's home was about as nice as a place made of garbage could be. It was surprisingly roomy, with several cots and a large stove. A series of maps and charts hung on the walls, making it feel more like a war room than a home.

Amanda brought out a basin filled with clean water, some towels, and bandages. The girls began to help each of the men wash their facial wounds. No one was actually hurt too badly. Bobby's nose seemed to have had the worst blow. It was beginning to swell and turn a deep purplish color.

"I'm really terribly sorry," said Amanda. She patted Tommy's busted upper lip with a wet towel. "We've been waiting for an attack from the Phantom Messengers, so when we heard you at the door of our tree house, we set our emergency plan in motion."

"It was a good plan," said Bobby. "At least now you know it works. But how is it you call this place a tree house?" He looked around the room. "Where's the tree?"

Amanda looked at Bobby, then over to Roger. "Well . . . we believe that some places that don't have trees still need tree houses. We didn't even have this place here until a few weeks ago. The way I see it, a tree house is simply a team on a mission from the Prince, whether the walls have been built yet or not."

"You are about like I remember you," said Tommy.

"Just a little taller," she said with a quick grin.

"And stronger." Tommy smiled, then winced as his lip cracked open again.

"We've been training as soldiers for a while now. The Prince sent us here a few months ago on a twofold mission: to build the first tree house in Gehin, or Zakum, whatever you call it, and also to prepare a battle plan to attack the furnace in the Pseudo."

"The Pseudo?" asked Tommy.

"Those are old-world names for things." Roger bandaged a small cut on his left hand. "Gehin is old-world for Zakum, and Pseudo was the old name of Senkrad's palace. Many years ago, before it was destroyed and rebuilt, it looked very much like the King's palace in the Upper Kingdom—only smaller, and less, well, just less. Thus the name."

"Haven't you taught them about the old world?" Amanda asked Roger.

"Not all, my dear. There just wasn't time. I'm afraid their training was severely cut short."

Amanda took a deep breath. "Well, here's what we do know: even though the Long Night is utterly black, we can actually see because of Samantha's ring of vision, a gift she received from the Prince before we came here."

"We have a ring as well," said Roger. Bobby raised his left hand to show the green jewel.

"Great," said Amanda. "That means we can split up. Samantha, go get the vials—all six of them."

"Vials of what? Poison?" Bobby looked at the young women with a mixture of amazement and admiration.

"Poison?" repeated Amanda. "I guess it's kind of like poison for Senkrad, but for us it may very well be the antidote. We have six small glass vials full of water from the River—from as close as we could get to its origin near the Palace of the Great King in the Upper Kingdom. From one of the stories of the ancients, we have hope that just one vial of water from the heart of the River will extinguish the fire in the furnace forever."

"The trick is just getting it in there," Samantha said, returning with the six small crystal tubes. She very carefully handed one to each person in the house. "Now we can go back to our original plan, Amanda."

"That's what I was thinking too," she replied.

"What was your original plan?" asked Tommy.

"We crossed over with three others, but they were . . ." Kelly stumbled over her words. "They . . . um—"

"They turned," said Amanda. "Within the first three days, they turned to the evil prince. Building a tree house in Gehin is . . . confusing. A person can lose touch with reality being this far away from the River. It's easy to become deceived."

"Where are they now?" asked Tommy. "The three who turned?"

"We don't know," Amanda replied. "We think they are in the

Pseudo. Maybe they have died. To be truthful, it doesn't really matter at this point. We could talk all day about this terrible war we are in, or we could fight today to end it. Here's our plan: Three of us should allow ourselves to be captured, while the other three hide out in one of the abandoned buildings near the Pseudo. Those of us who are captured can smuggle in the vials of water. The best-case scenario is that one of us is enslaved near the furnace after our capture. I mean, it could just be that easy. We get in and put out the fire and get out."

"What's the worst-case scenario?" asked Bobby.

"They kill us all," answered Samantha bluntly.

"Or they capture us and chain us in the dungeon with no hope of escape," added Roger.

"What will the other three of us do—those who aren't captured?" asked Tommy.

"They will wait exactly twelve hours after the first three are captured. At that time, they can cause a disturbance at the guarded entry. Hopefully, one of us inside will be close enough to get a vial into the fire by then, if the other guards rush to the gate or get distracted during the disturbance. If not, then the rest of us will also be captured. That means at the very least, we'd have six people with vials in the building."

"So, who's going in?" asked Bobby. "I think I should go—I'm not afraid."

"I'm going in," said Amanda. "I'm trained to fight them—it's what I do."

"And I will go. It's why I'm here," Tommy offered.

"Your jacket will help too. A humility jacket, right? They'll know what it means. It may open doors for us."

"How's that?" Bobby asked.

"They will assume he is special—that he knows something. It could mean that they will torture you mercilessly; or it could mean that you will be treated as some sort of ambassador or dignitary. Either way, it will take some of the attention off Bobby and me while we try to get close to the fire."

Tommy fumbled with the buttons on his jacket, taking some time to fasten each one. Then he stood up and rubbed his neck, glancing at Roger. "Is this OK with you Roger? This plan?"

He nodded. "This war is yours to win now. I got you here. You get us home."

"Then it's a plan," said Tommy.

"It's a plan," they all said in solemn unison.

To the Captors

"**H**ux, insid. Ferut, ferut . . ." His forked tongue slipped from his mouth, dropping a wad of saliva onto his breastplate. He wore a bronze helmet with a blue, transparent eye guard covering his face. His lizard-like tale whipped from side to side as he stood guard at the main entrance to the Palace of the Dark Prince.

Through his visor he could see clearly in the Long Night. He scanned the city for anything that seemed out of the ordinary. Since the Long Night had begun, he scarcely saw anyone moving at all in the city streets, let alone someone who would dare to threaten his lord, Senkrad the Great.

He straightened himself in surprise as three mysterious figures in hooded black robes walked boldly down the road leading to the front door of the palace.

"Hus! Hus!" he yelled at the top of his voice. Two other guards, bigger yet, exited the front door of the palace, standing at his right and left. They held enormous wooden clubs embedded with flat, sharp-edged stones, and they wore visored helmets as well.

"At least it's a fair fight—three on three," whispered Amanda from her position in the middle of the trio.

"This could hurt a lot." Tommy's voice came from deep within his hooded robe.

The three children of the King walked straight up to the guard creatures. In a seemingly unending moment, they stood staring at one another in silence. Then Amanda removed her hood and spoke in a loud voice, "We are here to see your lord and master. We have a secret message from our King."

"Hus. Basiped?" asked the first guard, looking to the monsters at his right and left.

"Basipeden, lix orn staidai!" said the one to his right before releasing a series of snorts and laughter.

"Flogan stei tran, Senkrad ton Gark," replied the girl. Tommy and Bobby watched in amazement. She confidently stared at the lead guard, awaiting his reply. He was more surprised than the boys to hear his native tongue from her lips.

"Stazen?" he asked.

"Stazen? Staze coa yehwa ton solon," she said, smiling victoriously. The vile creature stared at her in shock. She stared back at him, lifting her eyebrows with a confident self-assurance. Just when Tommy and Bobby thought that Amanda had managed to talk her way into the palace, the middle guard whispered some indistinguishable word to his companions.

The two clubs came straight for their heads.

Thump . . . thump . . . thump . . . thump.

Keys rattled just outside the heavy iron door.

"Here he comes," whispered Pops. "You ready?"

"Yes," whispered Mary from within the burlap sack covering her head.

Pops heard the skeleton key slide into the lock, releasing the dungeon's door, accompanied by a series of snorts and mumblings from the doorkeeper. Walking straight to Pops, he dropped a plate of rotting food at his feet. Then he fumbled with his keys again and unlocked Pops's left hand so that he could eat.

As he turned, Pops lifted the blindfold with his free hand just enough to see him. He wasn't a Phantom at all, but a man. At least he seemed mostly a man. Short and hunched over, but with strong, wide shoulders. He wore a dirty shirt with a leather vest. His greasy black hair flowed out from a leather helmet on his head. He snorted and mumbled again as he dropped Mary's plate at her feet.

"You're not what I expected to see," said Pops, before he fully removed his blindfold.

The doorkeeper pivoted on his heels and snapped back at Pops, "Shezin, basiped!"

"Speak to me in your own language," said Pops. He calmly selected an apple core from his plate and began to eat.

The man creature looked back at Pops uncomfortably.

"Come on, speak to me in the King's language. I know that you still know it." Pops smelled the moldy bread and ate some of the crust that seemed most palatable. "Go on, what is your name? How did you get here? How can we get out of this place?"

The man turned in anger back to Mary and unbound her hands. Then he untied the rope around her neck and quickly removed the covering from her head, accidentally ripping off the scab above her wounded eye. Blood immediately flowed into her left eye, down her nose, and into her mouth. She spat blood on the plate of rotting food.

"Sorry," grunted the guard.

"Aha!" yelled Pops. "Now you've done it. You've outed yourself. Go on, then—your name?"

"Thanaton," he said looking at the ground in defeat.

Pops shook his head. "No, not that name. What was your real name?" Mary tried to clean up her bloody face with a piece of the sack that had been on her head.

"That is my name now," he said.

"What's your name, son?" asked Pops. "What does the King call you?"

"Stop it! You are the captive. I'll ask the questions here," he snorted again and turned back to deal with Mary.

"Hurry up and eat so I can tie you up. I'll leave the bag off your head if you cooperate," he said.

She looked up at him, bloody, but smiling. "My name is Mary. What's your name?"

He grew frustrated with them both. "Don't. Don't—don't try to—"

"Know your name?" she persisted.

In anger he went for the burlap sack to cover her head again. As he bent over beside her, Mary ripped the locket from her neck, opened it, and held it out in front of her captor's face.

He pulled himself up, staring at the locket. "What's that?"

Mary sat motionless, with her arm frozen in the air. Pops watched nervously. The man tilted his head and bent back over the tiny mirror. He gazed at the image staring back at him. Though he looked the same to Pops and Mary, the mirror revealed a seven-year-old boy with a dark-haired crew cut, dimples, and sparkling hazel eyes. The boy in the reflection wore the same leather helmet as the dungeon master. He touched his own face with his filthy hand to see the image copy his action. Tears formed in his eyes.

"Now, what's your name—your real name?" Mary whispered.

"Joey," he whispered back.

"How long have you been here, Joey?" asked Pops, gently.

He never broke his staring match with the child in the mirror. "Way too long," he mumbled. "I don't know for sure. Just way too long."

"Are you ready to go home?" asked Mary.

"They won't take me back."

"Who won't take you back?" asked Pops.

"Amanda and the girls," he said.

Pops leaned forward as far as his one chained arm would allow him to move. "Well, I don't know who this Amanda is, but I can tell you one thing—the Great King and the Good Prince *will* take you back. Trust me, I know."

Joey finally broke his gaze. He wiped his eyes and walked slowly back to the dungeon door. Pops and Mary watched in silence as he fully opened the door and extended his head into the interior passageway, looking to his right and left. Then he pulled his body back into the cell and softly closed the door, locking it from the inside with his key. Without speaking, he walked first to Pops and opened all of his shackles. Then he loosed the remaining ropes that had bound Mary.

Once they were both freed, he sat against the dungeon wall, looked up at the two of them, and asked, "What do we do now?"

The Furnace Room

The Palace of the Dark Prince of the Lower Kingdom had long boasted a tall golden watchtower extending high into the clouds. This repurposed watchtower now served as the smokestack for the fiery furnace that created the evil, black smoke of the Long Night. The furnace itself was bigger than two double-story tree houses, and it was so hot that neither the Phantoms nor the men and women enslaved by them could get within thirty paces of its fire without melting or bursting into flames.

Wood from trees and tree houses from all over the Lower Kingdom was constantly being carted into the furnace room on the Phantom barrows. Enslaved children of the King unloaded the carts while others placed the wood on a series of screeching metal conveyors that carried it up to higher and higher levels, eventually dropping the wood into the flames of the furnace several stories above their heads. A horde of Phantom slave drivers beat with leather whips any of the children who faltered from the task they were assigned. From time to time, a slave would venture too close to the furnace or conveyor mechanism and become terribly injured. The severely wounded were carted off in the outgoing barrows and dumped in the trash heaps of Zakum where they were left to die. A wounded Phantom, however, would be thrown immediately onto the conveyors by his own people and consumed by the fire.

It had been about six hours since Bobby had been beaten, stripped of his hooded robe, and dragged into the furnace room. He was placed on cart duty as soon as he regained consciousness. His head bore an open wound from the Phantom's strike. The blood loss had left him disoriented and confused; so much so that he had nearly convinced himself that he was only having a terrible nightmare. He was chained to two other slaves by a snorting and spitting Phantom.

"Basiped, fut," mumbled the Phantom, as he shackled Bobby's left foot to the right foot of an older man with a short gray beard.

"Just let him do it," said the man, in a weary voice. "There's no way around it."

"How long have you been here?" asked Bobby.

"Don't know . . . I lost track," he said.

"Hut!" barked the Phantom. He rose and stood in the face of the older man. "Hut! Hut!"

"Sorry," the man whispered instinctively to his slave master.

The Phantom squatted again and shackled Bobby's other foot, attaching it to a younger lady's leg at his right side. She was so covered in grease from the conveyors, Bobby couldn't tell the color of her skin or hair. She looked at him for a moment, then quickly stared back at the ground. Bobby scanned the entire furnace room looking for Amanda and Tommy. He saw countless slaves working, but no one looked familiar—except for a few people in torn and soiled tuxedos, whose faces he recognized from Simon's house. Once his chains were fixed, the Phantom led the threesome down a corridor by a chain leash around the older man's neck. He brought them to a wooden horse cart filled with lumber and tree limbs. He pointed with one of his taloned fingers and said, "Uhn-lowd!"

The man and woman unloaded the lumber, placing it awkwardly on a nearby conveyor. Bobby stood motionless as he tried to understand exactly what he was being asked to do. As a result, he took a leather whip on the back from his slave master. "Uhnlowd!"

Bobby winced and moved toward the cart. As he unloaded the fuel for the fire, he felt under his belt for the vial of water from the River. It was gone. That's also when, to his great dismay, he felt his naked ring finger. His gift was also gone.

"Keep working," whispered the timid girl attached to him. She looked up at him with her dirty face and deep-set, dark eyes. "Just keep working. The Great King watches. He moves."

"She'll talk your ear off, boy," said the old man. "She's a little crazy."

Bobby looked back at the girl and winked. She did not acknowledge him, but whispered, "He's coming . . ."

Madam Alu

T he room contained nothing except a lone torch on the wall and an old but sturdy wooden chair, which was bolted in the middle of the floor. The chair was equipped with various clamps and straps that, once fastened properly, could render a person completely unable to move.

Amanda was placed in the chair with her head, torso, hands, arms, legs, and feet strapped and clamped down—so tightly that her fingers and toes almost immediately began to tingle with the loss of circulation. She first heard a scratch at the door, followed by the clang of keys and the unlatching of the lock. Light from the dungeon's corridor spilled in as the heavy iron door creaked open.

"Here you are, Madam Alu," said a male voice.

"That's fine. I can handle it from here," the lady replied.

"Very well, I'll come back to lock the door when you leave," said the keyholder.

Through the light from the corridor, Amanda saw a tall woman with long black hair, dressed in a flowing red gown that swirled around her feet with every step she took. She had a perfect physical form, and though shadows hid her face, Amanda was at once struck by her enchanting beauty.

The lady slowly walked to the middle of the room, her high-heeled boots landing on the stone floor with a rhythmic *click, click, click*. She stopped just in front of the chair and looked down at Amanda without emotion. Her hair framed her face beautifully, falling down in soft waves over her left shoulder. The subtle aroma of her intoxicating perfume filled the tiny room.

"Hello there, Amanda," she purred.

"How do you know my name?"

"I know just about everything about you, Amanda. Everything except why someone as smart as you would allow yourself to be so easily captured."

Amanda looked away with her eyes, just about the only part of her she could still move freely.

"Look at me when I talk to you, dear. Why do you want to be here so badly?" asked the lady.

"I don't want to be here at all. I'd just as soon leave if it's all the same to you."

"Do you know who I am?" the lady asked, as she slowly removed her elbow-length, black leather gloves.

"No. Should I?" Amanda couldn't help smiling a little.

"Yes, you should. Someone as studied and prepared as you should know all about me. Maybe you know me by one of my other names, but you may just call me Madam Alu if you want."

"What do you want from me?"

"I'm not the one who came into your home, my dear, you came into mine. I'm the one who will ask the questions. And you, sweet girl, will answer. Now, what do *you* want from *me*?"

"I want the Long Night to end."

Alu smiled. "Is that all? Well, I'll talk to my master and see what I can do for you," she said, with an acidic smile. Her sarcastic tone turned harsh and cold. "Now, about your intrusion. I have to decide if I want to kill you now or keep you around as a little trophy to help my master in the future."

"I'm not afraid of you, and I'm not afraid to die. Do what you must," said Amanda, lifting up her chin.

Alu wrinkled her nose and flashed her teeth like a wild beast. Her open mouth exposed two extremely long and sharp canines. As she spoke, she seemed to growl. "Rrrr . . . rrrreallly? Well, you should be afrrraid. Verrry afrrraid." Her pupils turned to flames of fire and the enchanting beauty in her face quickly faded away.

Amanda shook her head, trying to make sense of what her eyes were seeing. Alu pounced on top of Amanda with a crazed ferocity. "Why arrre you herrre?" she growled. With her sharp teeth only an inch from Amanda's immobilized face, Amanda could do nothing but close her eyes. Her attacker's breath smelled like rotten flesh, and it mixed with her sweet perfume to create a nauseating concoction. Amanda pressed her lips together and swallowed hard, trying not to vomit.

Alu began to sniff Amanda's neck and arms like a dog, moving down her body until she caught scent of something in her pants pocket. Reaching her hand into Amanda's pocket, she removed the vial and leaped backward off of her.

"What is this, little girl?" the crazed creature asked, holding the vial in Amanda's face.

"Nothing," replied Amanda. "Just water."

"What is it?" she howled, causing her face to lose all that was left of its beauty. Amanda watched curiously as the woman's nose turned black and wet, and long whiskers began to grow from the corners of her upper lips.

"It's a magic potion," Amanda said.

Alu tilted her head, and Amanda thought that she saw one of her ears actually grow longer and flop over itself.

Every word from the morphing woman now sounded more like a bark, "Whut! Duz! It! Doh?"

Amanda pretended to be worn down and afraid. "It gives to the one who drinks it ultimate power," she answered, with some struggle. "If only I had been able to drink it myself before being captured!"

That was all that Alu needed to hear. She fumbled with the vial in an attempt to open it with her hands that were now more like paws. In her clumsy effort, she dropped it and the crystal shattered on the stone floor. A puddle of River water formed on the ground. Frenzied, Alu fell to all fours and lapped the water from the ground. As soon as the water touched her lips she transformed completely into a large and ferocious black dog—an unearthly mammoth breed. She continued to lap up the liquid, and the more she drank, the smaller she became.

Just as the River takes years off the aged children of the King, so it turned Senkrad's evil guard dog into a seven-week-old puppy. If Amanda had not been tied to the chair, she could have picked up the former Madam Alu and held her with one hand. The pup, now exhausted, hopped over to Amanda's feet, curled itself into a ball, and slept.

Amanda sat staring at the wall in a haze. Her vial had saved her life in this moment, but now it was unavailable for her primary mission. After a few minutes, Amanda heard the keys at the door again. She braced herself for the worst. The door creaked open and a distorted face peered through.

"Madam Alu? Are you all right?" asked the keyholder.

"She isn't here," replied Amanda. "I killed her."

The door opened wider to reveal a short and stocky man with long hair and a leather helmet. As he opened the door, the puppy ran to him and sniffed his feet. He looked back into the corridor and motioned with his head for his companions to join him. Two others entered the room, an older man and a pretty, but wounded young lady. She closed the door behind them and the keyholder locked them all in from the inside.

The old man looked to the keyholder and nodded. The man in the helmet walked up to Amanda, with the puppy following at his heels. Once in the light of the hanging torch, Amanda recognized her old friend.

"Joey?"

"Forgive me, Amanda," he said, with tears running down both cheeks. "I'm so sorry. I was weak."

Her throat tightened. "I forgive you. Of course, I forgive you. You're not going to hurt me now, are you?"

"No, I'm here to save you. Or, I should say, *we* are here to save you."

Amanda noticed the other figures as they walked into the light. The older man spoke for both of them. "Hi, Amanda. My name is Freddie, but my friends call me Pops. This is Mary. We are children of the Great King like you. We need to work together to end this thing."

Amanda looked at Joey, who nodded in agreement.

"Do you know where Tommy is?" asked Mary.

Amanda shook her head. "He's in here somewhere, and so is Bobby."

The Other Prince

Tommy found himself in the middle of a huge bed covered with a thick, white, down comforter. The room was bright, and if he had not known better, he would have thought that the sun was shining in through the many windows. Touching his head, he discovered that his wound had already been neatly bandaged. He also realized that he was now wearing white, silk pajamas. His hooded robe was gone, as were his clothes—including his jacket. He sat up in a panic.

A man sat in an easy chair across from him. The man had his legs crossed casually and was sipping tea from a cup. He had a sparkle in his eyes and a kind, relatively young face. Though Tommy had never seen him before, the man seemed strangely familiar to him.

"How's your head, Tom?" the gentleman asked.

"Do I know you?" asked Tommy.

"Search your heart. I think you do," replied the mysterious man. He stood up from the chair and walked over to a small bar. He poured freshly squeezed orange juice from a glass pitcher into a tall, chilled glass and brought it to Tommy.

"Drink this. Your breakfast is on its way." Tommy sat on the edge of the bed, looking suspiciously at the orange juice.

"Tom—or Tommy, if you prefer—if I had wanted to hurt you

or poison you I would have done it already. Drink your juice. Two gentlemen ought to be able to trust each other, yes?"

Tommy was parched and he gulped the juice down. It was the best-tasting drink he had ever had in his life. The man returned to his chair and crossed his legs once more.

"Would you like some more?" He asked, with friendly eyes.

Tommy shook his head no. "Are you . . . Senkrad?"

The man laughed. "Senkrad? No. There is no Senkrad, my brother. It's all a very silly myth. My name is Adam. This is my home."

The man seemed so familiar to Tommy, like an old friend or relative. It was making Tommy crazy as he tried to place his face.

"I'm confused," Tommy admitted. "Where are Amanda and Bobby?"

"They are being helped by some of my friends, Tommy," said the man. "How about you think about yourself for a change? Why did you come here in such a hostile manner? I would have been happy to invite you in and discuss things, like two reasonable, well, adults. I don't understand why you wouldn't give me a chance to be your friend, before deciding to make me an enemy." He almost sounded hurt.

"I didn't just decide to make you my enemy, Sen—Adam. You are the one who started all of this. If you really are the prince of this world, then you owe us all an explanation. You made the Long Night, not us," said Tommy.

"A prince is the son of a King, Tommy. I'm not a prince. I am no one's son."

"So you are a king, then?" asked Tommy.

"I don't like to think of it that way," said the man, with another friendly smile. "I'm really more of a servant than anything else. I serve everyone who lives in the Lower Kingdom. Think of me as the Servant-in-Chief."

"How is all of this darkness and destruction serving these people?" Tommy swung the covers off and sat up in the bed.

The man looked steadily into Tommy's eyes. "How old do you think I am, Tommy?"

"I don't know. What does it matter?"

"Take a guess. How old do I look?"

"Maybe thirty," said Tommy.

"I'm twenty-nine," he said. "I have been in this Kingdom for hundreds of years, but I'm only twenty-nine. Eternally twenty-nine."

"I don't understand your point," said Tommy.

"I know how old you are. You are seven. You look like you could be my age, but you aren't, are you? You must be embarrassed of your real age down here in my world; and I understand why. What does a seven-year-old know about life? About death? About trust or wisdom or anything of any importance? Don't misunderstand me, Tommy. It's not your fault you don't know many things . . . most seven-year-olds simply aren't that informed yet. Don't you ever want to grow up a little, Tommy? Don't you ever want to know a little more? To be . . . older?"

Tommy rubbed his forehead. Was this all a bad dream?

"Tommy? I asked if you ever want to be older?"

"I don't know . . . maybe I'd like to be older sometimes, but I know I don't want to die, and old people eventually die."

"That's where you're wrong, Tommy," Adam placed his teacup on the table beside his chair and leaned forward. In a near whisper, he continued, "I'm still alive. I haven't died. I've found the perfect age and stayed there. A few years older than this and my body would start to break down ever so slightly. I'd become just a little weaker day by day, until my body would eventually wear out, as you say. A few years younger than this and I wouldn't be as strong and mature as I am right now. This is the perfect age, and I wish everyone could be twenty-nine forever. That's all I'm trying to do . . . just help people live better lives. Share what I know, what I have."

"But how did you do it? How did you get to this age and then stop growing?"

"I willed it. You can too, Tommy. You can . . . most people can't. Most people need someone like us to will it for them. That's what the Long Night is all about. The sun is what ages my people, you see. Those harmful rays. I'm trying to stop them from aging. Once I do, I have a plan to bring light back into the world. I wouldn't leave those I love in darkness forever. Not like your King has done to you."

"My King would never keep me in darkness," snapped Tommy.

"Oh, well, I mean no offense. He gives you light for your eyes, yes, but what about your mind? He keeps the important things from you, Tommy. Tell me, what has your King taught you about the mystery of death? Has he told you anything about death, except that you should avoid it? What has he told you about the messengers? What about the ocean that surrounds the island? Where does it go? What is its name? What of the stars, Tommy? Where did they come from? Where do they go when night fades? What has he taught you about how these two kingdoms were formed? Who created them in the first place? Surely, someone did? What has he done for you except make you a leader and force you to wear a ridiculous coat that actually prevents you from leading well?"

Tommy sat on the edge of the bed, motionless, yet feeling pulled in a thousand directions. "I feel sick."

Just then there was a knock on the door.

"Come in," said the monarch.

Tommy could not believe what he saw next. The most beautiful creature he had ever beheld entered the room. A true messenger came through the doors. He was tall and slender, dressed in a gray robe with a golden sash and boots. He wore a silver crown on his head and a sword hung from his waist. In his hands he carried a golden tray filled with eggs, sausages, fruits, breads, and pastries. He placed it on the bed next to Tommy with a nod of his head. Looking to his master, he bowed and asked, "Is that all, my lord?"

"That's fine, Draxon. Off you go now."

Tommy had no appetite after seeing the messenger. He had so many questions, but asked none of them.

"Amazing, aren't they? They just keep coming, Tommy. They get bored with the so-called Upper Kingdom and seek a more interesting life. They show up every day, sometimes by the dozens. I don't go looking for them. They come to me, because I have answers to the questions they aren't allowed to ask your King."

"So you take beautiful messengers and turn them into Phantoms?" Tommy asked.

"Phantoms? They are vile and ugly, aren't they? I do feel sorry for them. They come to me after your King makes them that way." Adam rose from his seat and examined a landscape painting on the wall. "If a messenger fails in any task—something as small as being a second late when your King summons him—he curses them and makes them ugly, black creatures. He dumps them in Gehin, and I pick them up to try to restore them to health." He motioned to the door, "Draxon, the one you just met, was a Phantom when I first dug him from the trash heap. Now, as you have seen, he is beautiful again. Maybe I'm naive, but I just believe everyone deserves a second chance."

"I don't feel well. I don't want to talk anymore. I just want to see my friends," Tommy admitted. "Do you know where Mary and the others are?"

Adam sat down by Tommy, a look of concern on his face. "Yes, I know all that happens in my Kingdom. Mary is in the dungeon. She tried to hurt my people, but we kept her alive; if for no other reason, hoping that you might come looking for her, and we could then have this interesting conversation. Fred, the man you call "Pops," is also there. Your friend Amanda is being questioned now. She may have to endure some pain, but it is for your sake that we know what she knows. Bobby is here too. He is being cared for by my team of doctors. All of them can be saved, Tommy. It is up to you."

"What do you mean?"

He folded his arms and leaned back, getting a better view of his guest. "I'll do whatever you want with them. I'll escort them back to the River or lead them myself to the Gate of Separation, if, for some reason, you want them to go back to that dreaded place. Or," he stood again, pacing across the room with his hands behind his back, "if you wish, I'll create positions in my leadership council for them. They can stay here and rule with you. Say the word."

"Rule with *me*?" asked Tommy.

"That's right. You are a leader, aren't you? Like I said, you are special. You can will your age. You can help me save all these people—if only you would be willing to put the needs of an entire kingdom above your selfish desires to protect yourself and your friends. Be a good leader."

A good leader, a good leader. What does that mean? "I don't know," Tommy said. He felt so uncomfortable, so vulnerable. Naked. Naked! His jacket! He needed his jacket!

The Dark Prince moved over to a desk, pulling open a drawer. He removed the vial of water that was discovered in Tommy's pocket.

"What is this, Tommy?" he asked.

Tommy didn't know what to say. Adam set the vial down on the desk. "It burns my hand when I touch it, Tommy. Is it what I think it is?"

"What do you think it is?" asked Tommy.

"The River." He tapped the top of the vial, being careful not to disturb the contents. "Do you know what the River really is, Tommy?"

Tommy shook his head to say no.

"It's liquid ignorance. Many of my people think that the River is nothing more than water. They are wrong about that. Your people are actually more correct in believing that it is powerful, but you are also deceived about its true identity. The River soothes people to death, Tommy. It makes you quit asking questions. It kills your brain. It makes you believe that life is simple and easy. Life is not simple and easy. But you know that, don't you."

Adam picked up the vial again. "What were you going to do with this?"

"Put it in the furnace." He just wanted this interview to be over.

The Dark Prince laughed. "Well, that would be an interesting little experiment, though probably much more trouble than it would be worth."

"I am cold," said Tommy. "May I have my jacket back now?"

"Your clothes are there in the closet." He pointed across the room. "But I have a new coat for you in there. The old one is cursed."

"If it's all the same, I'd like to have mine back," replied Tommy.

"It's not all the same, Tommy. I destroyed your coat before it destroyed you. You will thank me later."

Tommy went to the walk-in closet and closed the door behind him. He silently removed his pajamas and put his old clothes back on. They had been washed, and smelled nice and clean. He hated that he liked the way they smelled. Somehow the darkness of the closet felt safer than the fake light of the bedroom. He needed that jacket. Surely that man didn't really destroy it? Could he do that?

"Are you all right in there, Tommy?"

Tommy thought quickly. He came here to save his friends, and to stop the Long Night. And that's what he would do. Without opening the door, he responded, "Here is my offer. I want all of my friends—Mary, Pops, Bobby, Roger, Luke, Amanda, and anyone else I may choose, delivered safely through the Gate of Separation. I also want the Long Night stopped immediately. I want you to promise never to enter the Tree House Village for any reason ever again . . . then I will do anything you ask." He took a deep breath. "I'll stay here with you as long as you want."

The Dark Prince smiled. "It's a deal, my friend. I can't say that I agree *with* your terms, but I will agree *to* your terms."

"Good! It must all happen today or the deal is off," said Tommy, buttoning up the new jacket left in the closet for him. It was deep purple and looked like something a king or prince would wear.

It fit him very well.

Two Lost and Two Found

Bobby was stationed so close to the furnace that he felt like his entire body was actually on fire. He and those chained to him were still throwing boards onto a conveyor. They'd been doing this for hours.

A short man came up to the Phantom slave driver in charge of Bobby and spoke to him in his language. The man pointed toward Bobby, then the Phantom came over and unlocked the shackles on his ankles. The Phantom put a chain leash around Bobby's neck and handed it to the man, who appeared to be some sort of supervisor.

"You're comin' with me now," said the man. He gave a firm tug on the chain and Bobby followed him. Over his shoulder he saw the Phantom beating the old man and younger woman previously attached to Bobby.

"Where are you taking me?" asked Bobby.

"Don't talk," said the man. He led him through a series of secret passageways and stairways leading down into the dungeon. The deeper they walked into the palace's underbelly, the fewer people Bobby saw. Eventually they were isolated in a narrow corridor. The man released Bobby's leash and unlocked an iron door to reveal a small room on the other side. At first, Bobby noticed the tiny black puppy that trotted over to his feet and started nipping at his shoelaces. Then he looked up to see Pops, Mary, and Amanda seated on the floor in front of an old wooden chair. Mary screamed for joy and jumped up and kissed both his cheeks. He lifted her up by the waist as he hugged her.

"You're alive!" she yelled.

"*Shhh!*" warned Joey as he closed the door behind him, still holding the chain leash in his hand.

"So, you're with us?" Bobby asked his leash holder, as he returned Mary to the floor.

"I'm Joey," he said. "I was part of Amanda's team and now I'm part of yours."

Pops stood and walked to Bobby, giving him a huge bear hug.

"Where's Luke?" asked Bobby.

"As far as we know, he's still protecting the village," answered Pops. "Mary and I were captured, but he wasn't."

"What about Tommy? Have you seen him?" asked Pops.

Bobby shook his head. "I don't know where he is. He wasn't in the furnace room. I have no idea." He looked over to Amanda and nodded.

"I don't have my vial anymore. I had to use it for something else. How about you?"

"No," said Bobby. "They took it from me—along with my ring. I didn't even have a chance to try to use it."

Suddenly a dragging noise and the familiar heavy footsteps of several Phantoms came from the corridor outside of the room.

"Thanaton! Basipeden!" one of them yelled from the hallway with a series of snorts.

"They're calling for me," said Joey. "I'll be right back!" He slipped through the door so that Bobby and the others could only hear a mumbled conversation through the walls. Amanda stood and walked to the door, trying to listen.

"I think they have more prisoners," she said. "I can barely hear what they are saying."

Before long, the Phantoms stomped away. Then the familiar sound of Joey's keys returned just outside of the door. It swung open as a prisoner flew in from the outside. He had been beaten, but was alive and alert. The door closed behind him and they could all hear Joey's voice yelling to someone in the Phantoms' tongue. He locked the door again.

The prisoner looked up at Pops who was directly in front of him. Both of his eyes were nearly swollen shut from his injuries, but he was able to spit out, "Freddie?"

"Roger! Is that you?" Pops fell to his knees and wiped the wounded face of his old friend.

Amanda rushed to his side. "Roger, are you OK? Do you still have your vial?"

Fumbling, he reached into his pants pocket and handed the container to Amanda. She inspected it and handed it to Pops. "This may be the last one we have," she advised Pops, as he carefully placed it in his coat pocket.

"Roger, where are Samantha and Kelly?" Amanda asked.

He looked up at Amanda and touched her face. "I'm not sure they made it," he said. "It was—really bad out there. I don't see how they could have made it."

Entering the Story

Luke watched everything carefully through the visor of the dead Phantom's helmet he wore. From his position behind the palace, he listened to the Phantom foreman bark out orders to others who waited to get their loaded carts full of wood into the watchtower. A backup had occurred, slowing down the flow of barrows in and out of the furnace room. Luke and Alex, disguised as Phantoms, were stuck outside in the traffic jam.

Had any of the Phantoms been a little more perceptive, they would have noticed that these two were obviously out of place. Not only were they a foot shorter than the shortest of them, but they wore heavy winter parkas covering their arms. Though they did wear sanctioned armor and helmets with visors, the closer the two imposters got to the watchtower entrance, the more out of place they seemed.

"I feel like this isn't going to work," Alex whispered through his faceguard.

"It'll work," said Luke. "Just play dumb if they talk to you."

Arriving at the delivery entrance, they were greeted by an incredibly fat man with missing teeth and a bushy brown moustache. He wore leather armor and spoke in the Phantoms' language. He actually spit more than he spoke.

"Haxthan kud?" he asked Luke.

He looked down without replying.

The fat man pointed to a pile of wood in the far corner of the furnace room, and raising his voice, he barked, "Kud!"

They pushed the cart inside and in that direction as he addressed the next group of incoming Phantoms, pulling a rickety horse cart full of tree limbs. The imposters slowly unloaded the cart as they scanned the room full of slaves.

On the other side of the room, Bobby stealthily navigated through the furnace room and found the girl who had been chained to his ankle hours earlier. She was now alone, chained to a metal grate in the conveyor system. Her assigned task was now to remove any large pieces of wood that might jam the system as the bins turned upward. Making eye contact with her from a crouched position behind the machinery, he held his finger to his mouth to silence her. Crawling on his belly with several of Joey's keys in his hands, he managed to unlock the shackles on her feet. Finally freed, she squatted down to speak with him. With joy in her eyes she asked, "Is he here?"

"Who?" whispered Bobby, as he motioned for her to get lower to the ground.

"The King?" she asked.

"No," said Bobby, "but his people are. Come with me."

Similar releases were occurring all around the perimeter of the furnace room as Joey dragged Mary and Amanda through the room in chains.

In the room with the solitary chair, Pops held the vial.

"Are you sure you want to come with me?" Pops asked Roger, who was now leaning against the cell wall. His left eye was completely swollen shut, but he could see well enough with the other. The puppy Alu slept, curled up, between his legs.

"Yes, I'm sure," he said. "What else would I do? Stay here with the cutest evil puppy in the world while you go down as a hero in the history books?"

Pops laughed. "I don't know about history . . ."

"You teach them about the Battle of Senkrad's Hill, about Apollon's legacy, about Etah's rise and fall. You taught me everything I know about this dark world. And the next recruits that come flowing down the River won't have you or me here to teach them. They'll have Luke or Mary or Bobby or—"

"Tommy. They'll have Tommy."

"OK then. Tommy will teach them about all of those important battles and amazing feats and huge personalities who wrote our story in the pages of time. He'll quiz them on all of it, and then on the last day of formal training, he will close his book and look at his students. He'll say, 'I have one more story to tell you and I don't need notes for this one because I was there.' He'll tell about this day. About us. About you, Pops. This is the day we stop telling the story and we enter the story. And there is no way I'm sitting down here with this dumb dog while you enter the story without me."

Pops stood and extended his hand to his friend to lift him to his feet. "Let's go do it then," he said.

Roger smiled and took his hand.

The Phantoms began to notice a lack of productivity. They ran around in circles screaming at one another and snorting. In the midst of the chaos, a Phantom ran past Amanda, who was now hiding behind a pile of wood that was waiting to be fed into the conveyor.

She tackled him, throwing a chain leash from one of the liberated slaves around his neck. She left him unconscious and chained him to the conveyor.

The two Phantom imposters, Luke and Alex, watched this happen and nodded to one another in agreement. They removed their parkas to reveal shirts fashioned with mirrors all over the fronts and backs. They both grabbed two hand mirrors from their pockets and walked from Phantom to Phantom, destroying them as they went, and leaving piles of black goo in their wake. They would occasionally rip mirrors from their shirts and give them to the freed slaves.

Amanda took a mirror from the shorter of the two. Standing back to back with him, they melted every Phantom who dared approach them.

"Who are you?" she called above the chaos.

"A Phantom killer," Luke responded back, still masked. "Who are you?"

"A tree-house builder," she said, as she melted one enemy with the mirror in her left hand and punched another with her right. It didn't take long for the strategy to spread throughout the furnace room. Before long there were actually more freed slaves than Phantoms.

The rioting emptied the guards from the dungeon hallways, allowing Pops and Roger to enter the furnace room unnoticed. Eyes squarely focused on the fiery furnace in the middle of the room, Pops turned to Roger with his face set like a stone. He reached into a pocket on the right side of his jacket and pulled out the wadded napkin with his cookie inside. "I'll wait on you," he said. Then he ran straight to the conveyor system, showing himself to several Phantoms. They immediately pursued him.

The conveyor mechanism was made of chains and a series of

huge metal bins that normally held the scraps of wood. Since so many slaves had been freed and were no longer working, many bins were now empty. Pops dove headfirst into one of them. It took him for a ride along the perimeter of the furnace, coiling up closer and closer to the fire as it went along.

Inside the bin, Pops dug through his coat pocket for the vial of water from the River. Holding the container in his hand caused his heart to long for her healing waters. He closed his eyes and could hear her song pushing and pulling him toward the fire above. Suddenly, the cart caught a large hook in the system, jolted, and made its final dramatic rise straight up toward the opening of the furnace. Pops peeked upward to see his fate. Soon he and the vial would be dumped like unwanted trash into the flames. From his position he could see everything happening below, including his recruits methodically destroying the evil Phantoms with their mirrors. The fire was so unbearable, that though he was still a considerable distance from the tipping point, his hands and face began to redden and blister. He just wanted it all to be over. He wanted to see his King again. He closed his eyes with the vial next to his face and began to repeat, "It's only a mask. It's only a mask."

Then, without warning, the entire conveyor system crashed to a dramatic halt. The furnace room filled with the grating noise of metal screeching against metal, mixed with the snorts and screams of the dying Phantoms. A booming voice echoed through the room, from the interior entrance to the watchtower.

"Silence!" demanded the Dark Prince of the Lower Kingdom.

All eyes turned to him. No less than thirty piles of melted Phantoms bubbled on the floor. The dozen or so Phantoms still living stopped and faced their supreme master with a salute. The prisoners, all unchained now, also turned from the battle to see what he would do. Amanda whispered to the Phantom imposter next to her, "Is that who I think it is?"

"I think so," he said, lifting his visor to reveal his black glasses and stringy hair. His partner, who had been fighting alongside Bobby, also removed his helmet. Bobby saw for the first time that it was Alex who stood beside him. They exchanged nods before looking back toward Senkrad as he stood in the entrance of the room.

Mary had recently found Roger during the battle. They stood together at the entrance to the secret hallway leading to the dungeon, watching Senkrad's every move.

Pops was so overcome by the heat in the stalled bin that he nearly fainted away. He was only three bins from the top of the furnace now, about thirty paces away. He pulled his jacket up around his face, using the collar to cover his mouth and nose. Old humility will keep me safe, he thought. Just keep me safe from the fire until I can do my job.

He shoved the vial back in his pocket and climbed from his cart, balancing himself precariously on the burning-hot track and chains. Unseen high above the crowds, he inched upward toward the next bin.

"Who is responsible for all of this?" asked the Dark Prince, who had now walked into the center of the loading area. He stood not far from Bobby and Alex. "No one wants to take responsibility?" he asked again. Then the fat man with the moustache from the outer entrance walked forward. He was bloody and battle-worn. "I tried to stop them," he said, falling before his master. "I tried."

"You tried?" Senkrad mocked him. "Really? It looks like you tried to destroy everything in here. You fat fool." Then he lifted the man up by his collar and threw him lightly into an empty bin on the conveyor belt.

"Anyone else want to take credit for this?" he asked, looking around at the destruction.

"Very well then, I'd like the following people to step forward." He looked back over his shoulder and nodded. Tommy entered. He wore his royal purple jacket and his hair was greased back and combed perfectly to one side. He stood beside the Dark Prince, surveying the room. As he saw his friends, he called their names and pointed to them, "Bobby . . . and Alex? Is that you?"

Alex nodded in the affirmative.

"OK, then . . . Alex," said Tommy. He continued to look through the crowd. "Amanda. Luke." His eyes strained to see. "Roger and Mary," he said, pointing in the shadows. "All of you, come to me now. You are going back to the other Kingdom." He searched the room for Pops, but could not find him.

"You had better do as he says," added the Dark Prince. "Before I change my mind." From all directions, Tommy's six friends slowly walked toward him. Mary was confused and troubled. She was the most cautious to come, and the last to arrive.

"What's going on, Tommy?" she asked.

He refused to look at her. He had never—not once since he had met her—refused to look at her before. He just couldn't bear to meet her eyes right now.

"Look at me, Tommy!" she protested.

But he would not. Instead, he shouted out: "Pops, where are you?"

Pops was nearing the final bin high above all that was happening. His hands were blistered and burned, and his long beard had been singed by the heat of the flames. His heavy jacket protected his torso, just as he had asked, otherwise he would have already succumbed to the intense heat and fallen to his death. He crawled into the top bin and, squinting through the opening in his jacket collar, saw the hungry flames in the heart of the furnace.

But somehow Tommy's question had made it to his ears. He had seen Tommy arrive with the Dark Prince, and knew something was amiss. He had not been able to discern exactly what was happening—he just had to focus on his task. But they couldn't stop him now.

He ducked his head down to the bottom of the bin and gathered some cooler air in his lungs. With all the strength he had left, he screamed, "Where's your jacket, Tommy?"

All eyes in the room, including Senkrad's, lifted to see the old man holding the vial of water and standing in the swaying bin.

"Get down, Pops!" Tommy yelled. "I've made a deal! You don't need to do this!" Tommy turned to Senkrad, "Tell him, Adam! Tell him that we made a deal."

"That's right, old man!" the Dark Prince laughed. "We have a deal! I'm going to shut down the furnace for a while—for maintenance," he said. "Clean out all the junk."

Tommy turned to his enemy, his face ashen. "What? No, I said you would shut it down forever. That was our deal."

"No you didn't, Tommy. You just said to shut it down immediately. I have already done that," said the Dark Prince. "We can't go changing the terms of the deal now . . . or else I'll have to kill your little friends."

"Don't do the deal, Tommy!" Mary pleaded.

"Quiet!" the Dark Prince shrieked, slapping her across the face with the back of his hand.

Tommy looked at Mary as she recoiled from the strike, blood dripping from her lip. Then he looked at his new master in confusion. Then, back up to Pops.

"He destroyed it, Pops!" he yelled. "He destroyed my jacket!"

"This is ridiculous," said the Dark Prince. "Go ahead! Kill yourself, you old imbecile! That bottle of insanity won't do anything but melt in my fire. Jump on in and die for nothing!"

Pops looked down with burning eyes, straight at Tommy. He unbuttoned his jacket and removed it for the first time in thirty years. Immediately he felt the full force of the flames on his body. With one motion he pulled the cap from the vial and threw his jacket down toward the gathered crowd below. Then he turned and heaved himself into the fire.

Mary covered her mouth in disbelief. Bobby picked up the jacket from the ground near him.

"I'll take that, boy," said Senkrad, reaching across Tommy toward Bobby.

"No," said Tommy. "You'll take this." He ripped off the purple coat, popping the gold buttons, and threw it at Senkrad's face. Bobby tossed him the old jacket, and he quickly put it on.

At that very moment, the fire within the furnace belched out a massive plume of white smoke, followed by a gush of water so intense, it shot out of the watchtower to more than 100 feet in the air. It mixed with the terrible black clouds in the sky and released a torrential rainstorm.

Cold water came rushing out of every hole and pore of the furnace, pushing back the metal walls and flooding the room. The water filled the room so quickly, no one had time to escape. Senkrad and his minions screamed as the water burned their skin like acid. The Phantoms dissolved into nothingness as soon as the waters touched them, but the allies of Senkrad rode the River in pain.

For it was the water of the River, come up from its underground path that meanders underneath the City of the Lower Kingdom. Those few drops in the vial were enough to burn a crack through the bottom of the furnace down deep into the earth, down where the River forms a spring, directly below the Palace of the Dark Prince of the Lower Kingdom.

The River flushed all through the palace and out the front entrance, picking up people as it went along. She filled the streets of the city and pushed all of them—hundreds of them now—toward the neglected building, which houses the rusty door, which is the Gate of Separation.

At the same time, the waters of the River at the banks of the Tree House Village reversed her flow. For the first time in recorded history of either Kingdom, the River flowed up the mountain, carrying every child of the King wading in her waters all the way to the backside of the Palace of the Great King.

The King Moves

The Great King had moved his throne to the grassy field beneath the Great Forest. He had it placed about three feet from the entrance of the gate separating Kingdom from Kingdom. He sat there and watched through the gate for several weeks as his children battled in the Lower Kingdom. The Good Prince stood beside him with his sword drawn, waiting for permission from his father to rescue the children trapped below. Behind the two of them, 10,000 messengers stood in formation ready for action. There was not a blade of grass in the entire field between the Great Forest and the gate that did not hold the shadow of a messenger waiting to rescue the King's children.

As the new River in the city flowed straight toward them, the King stood for the first time in weeks. When he stood, the Prince raised the Dunamas. Then all the messengers raised their swords, staring forward at attention. The Prince alone moved his face toward his father to await his orders. The King said nothing, but simply held out his right hand. In obedience, the River stopped in mid-flow, immediately tossing everyone in her waters onto the alley leading to the Gate of Separation, and forming a wall of water about twenty feet tall behind them.

From his position, the King watched the people struggling to their feet on the street below. He saw Tommy and Mary. He saw the girl who was previously chained to Bobby, and though no one knew her name, he did. He saw those captives from Simon's party in their drenched tuxedos. He saw Joey and Amanda and Roger and Luke. And he saw Senkrad, rubbing his eyes and vomiting water from the River onto the dry ground.

In one stride, the King was at the gate. He put each of his royal hands on a side of the gate separating Kingdom from Kingdom and clutched the bars. He bent at his knees and, with some effort, ripped its ancient foundations from the ground, lifting it straight above his head. A blinding light filled the entire Lower Kingdom, ending all that was left of the Long Night. Tommy, Mary, and everyone else on the street covered their eyes.

The King took one giant step toward them, carrying the gate high above his head. Then he took another step. And another. With each step, the Prince followed suit, just one step behind his father. All 10,000 of the messengers matched the Prince step for step. There were about 1,500 paces between where the gate had always been and where the King had ordered the River to halt. Though the gate was heavy beyond measure, the King continued to methodically take each and every step toward the River. As he moved along, he claimed every inch as his own. "This is the land of the Great King! And of his son, the Good Prince!"

He reclaimed land that the Great King had not occupied for centuries, since before the old world, since before the time of the ancients, since before any time that anyone had ever known. The borders between the two Kingdoms changed with each of his steps. As far as could be seen to his right and left, the King redeemed his land. The old and dirty buildings crumbled into the grassy meadow. The dusty streets became soft, green paths, littered only with toadstools and wildflowers.

As he stepped among the people, each person immediately turned into a seven-year-old child—even those who had forgotten all about the King. With one step, Bobby transformed back into a child. With the next, Mary and Roger. Then Joey, Amanda, and Alex. Then Luke. Then, finally, Tommy. The King kept walking until every adult was a child and every inch of land he wanted belonged to him again.

Now, Senkrad had backed himself up against the River's wall as the King advanced against him. He could see nothing in the light, but could feel the burn of the River on his back. He stayed there until he was the last creature left in what had been the Lower Kingdom. Only two paces remained and the King would have rightfully claimed all of the land between the gate and the River. The King spoke from the blinding light to his last, lost child.

"What do you want, Adam? Say the word."

"Make it stop!" he cried. "I want it to stop! Please!"

"Do you want me to come in?" asked the King.

"No! Please. The pain! Just make it stop," he cried.

"Two more steps. Two more steps, and you will be home," said the King.

"All I want is to be free. To be left alone. Please, give me one more chance. I know I can do it this time—just stop the pain!" He was pitiful beyond words.

"Very well," said the King. "You may live in the space between the River and the Light. I give it to you."

At his words, the Great King planted the gate in the ground at his feet.

The Light disappeared to reveal a giant wall of stone, six feet from Adam's face. The pain gradually left his body. He turned and found another stone wall where the River had been seconds earlier.

He was alone. The silence hurt his ears. He looked as far as he could to his right and to his left and then he looked up into the sky. In every direction, all he could see were the walls. They never ended.

This was now the kingdom of the Dark Prince.

He whispered, "Grattsin yehwa," and walked westward in hopes of finding the slither of Gehin left in his territory, and perhaps some interesting piece of trash there to keep him occupied for a while.

The First Breakfast

The sun that day was warm and bright. Though it had been three days since his return, Tommy's eyes were still not completely accustomed to the abundance of light in the Upper Kingdom. But he loved being seven again. It was even better than before.

The King had gifted to Tommy one of the new tree houses from his expanded territory. Tommy lived there with Bobby, Joey, and Luke. There was still plenty of room for Roger to move in whenever he was ready to make the trip down the mountain.

Amanda was granted an old hardware store, one of the few buildings from the old city that had not crumbled. With some help, she had transformed it into a gymnasium for training new recruits. She moved into the upper level alone, but had prepared three other rooms for some friends to move in with her. She hoped Mary would be one of them. Next to Amanda's gym, there was a small open-air vegetable stand with a humble apartment attached to it. It had previously been a bank in the Lower Kingdom. Alex and Campbell happily lived there as seven-year-old children.

A simple but intriguing log cabin had been birthed right next to where the King had planted the gate. The King had not yet given it to anyone, but from time to time the Prince himself would go inside. Tommy and the others would hear him hammering or sawing for a while, then he would leave with a wave and a smile.

This was a special morning because Mary and Roger were being released from the infirmary in the palace. Their wounds had healed enough to join the other children. Tommy walked through the Great Forest, up the mountain toward the palace with Joey. Joey went everywhere with Tommy, learning all that he could from him.

They exited the forest to see the palace before them. Children were running all around playing hide-and-seek in the garden. Tommy saw the Prince sitting at a large table with three familiar children: Bobby, Luke, and Amanda. Alex and Campbell were standing beside the table laughing and talking with two other girls whom Tommy did not recognize. Tommy approached them and everyone greeted him all at once. He smiled and waved, running up to the Prince.

"Hi, Tommy!" said the Prince with a huge smile. "It's a big day! We are all here!"

Tommy still wore Pops's jacket with the sleeves rolled up. It didn't fit him as a child at all, but he never removed it, not even to sleep. He waved to his friends and looked to the new girls. They seemed familiar, but he couldn't place their faces.

"Hi, Tommy!" one of them said. "It's us!"

"It's Samantha and Kelly," said Amanda. "They're OK!"

"I thought I recognized you," said Tommy. "I'm so glad you are here. Thanks for not hitting me this time!"

"They're moving into the gym with me," added Amanda.

"We'll be neighbors then. That's great—that will give me a chance to hear what happened to you in the Lower Kingdom," said Tommy.

"You'll never believe it, even when we tell you," laughed Samantha.

"Try me," said Tommy.

From behind Tommy, a seven-year-old Roger cleared his

throat. Tommy turned to see his old friend—now young again. They hugged. Roger still had a patch over his eye, but seemed well otherwise.

"Hi, Tommy," he said. "I brought a friend of yours with me." Mary stepped out from behind him and she looked exactly the way Tommy remembered her before the Long Night had begun. She smiled at him and he grabbed her and hugged her, harder than he ever had in his life. "I'm sorry, Mary, I'm sorry," he whispered over and over, as a few of his tears fell on her shoulder. She held him, crying too and saying, "It's OK, Tommy. It's OK."

The Prince rose from the table and put his arms around Tommy and Mary. He knelt and wiped the tears from their eyes. "It's over, Tommy. We are all here. We are all fine. I'm not upset with you and neither is Mary. You made some mistakes, but you did what I asked you to do. You led them all home."

"Not all," said Tommy sadly, and stuffed his hands into his jacket pockets.

"You all are gonna make this old man cry," said a squeaky child's voice, coming from behind Tommy.

Mary and Tommy turned their heads together to see a freckled boy smiling back at them. He had bandages on his hands, legs, and face.

"Pops?" they said, in disbelief.

"That's what my friends call me," he said. Then he was swarmed by the whole crowd of children. When the hugging and holding and crying had stopped, Pops sat down at the table. He looked up at Tommy, who wouldn't leave his side. "Nice jacket, Tommy."

Tommy began to unbutton it. "You can have it back. I was just keeping it warm for you."

"Keep it. I don't need it anymore. I'm staying here for a while, anyway. The weather's nicer up here."

"Keep it, Tommy," said the Prince. "Pops wants you to have it. So do I."

"There is just one thing I'd love to have back," said Pops. At that, he reached up to Tommy and opened the right front jacket pocket. He held up a small, napkin-covered bundle in his bandaged hand, then folded back the napkin and revealed his cookie. "It's breakfast time!" he said. "Anyone else have their cookie?"

"I have mine!" said Luke, pulling it from his pants pocket.

Tommy, Mary, and Bobby had lost theirs in the battle. Roger pulled his from his pocket as well.

"Three cookies should be enough for now. There's plenty more where these came from, after all." Pops gathered the cookies from Luke and Roger and handed them with his to the Prince. "You want to do the honors?" he asked.

"Sure, Freddie. Let's all have a seat at the table." The Prince began to break the cookies, giving everyone a bite. He walked around the table, touching each child on the head as he went. He gave a bite to Pops first, then Tommy, Mary, Bobby, Luke, Amanda, Samantha, Kelly, Joey, Alex, Campbell, and Roger. By the time he had completed the circle, only one bite of cookie remained.

"Just enough for all of us," the Prince said, as he lifted his bite into the air. "To my father," he said with a smile.

"To our King," the children responded with one voice.

The Good Prince and twelve of his most devoted followers ate their first breakfast together in the bright sun of the Upper Kingdom. They laughed and talked until the sun set behind the mountain. They had never, ever been happier.

But somewhere in another Kingdom, a desperate and lonely creature was beating a stone wall with a recently discovered rusty pickaxe.

"Basipeden, hux, hus, thanatan," he mumbled, in darkness and solitude, swinging the axe over and over and over.